Redemption

BETH SHRIVER

REALMS

Most Charisma House Book Group products are available at special quantity discounts for bulk purchase for sales promotions, premiums, fund-raising, and educational needs. For details, write Charisma House Book Group, 600 Rinehart Road, Lake Mary, Florida 32746, or telephone (407) 333-0600.

Redemption by Beth Shriver
Published by Realms
Charisma Media/Charisma House Book Group
600 Rinehart Road
Lake Mary, Florida 32746
www.charismahouse.com

Although this story is depicted from the town of Lititz, Pennsylvania, and the surrounding area, the characters created are fictitious. The traditions are similar to the Amish ways, but because all groups are different with dialogue, rules, and culture, they may vary from what your conception may be.

Cover design by Justin Evans

Visit the author's website at www.BethShriverWriter.com.

Library of Congress Cataloging-in-Publication Data
Shriver, Beth.
Redemption / Beth Shriver. -- First edition.
pages cm. -- (Spirit of the Amish ; 3)
ISBN 978-1-62998-602-9 (paperback) -- ISBN 978-1-62998-603-6 (e-book)
1. Amish--Fiction. I. Title.
PS3619.H7746R46 2014
813'.6--dc23

2015029373

First edition

15 16 17 18 19 — 9 8 7 6 5 4 3 2 1
Printed in the United States of America

Dedicated to Carrie Padget, the best critique partner an author could wish for.

Chapter One

Fannie paused at the top of the stairs as her *mamm*'s and *mammi*'s voices carried toward her from the kitchen. It was wrong to eavesdrop, but she gave into the temptation anyway. How could she resist listening when she was the topic of conversation?

"I'm quite sure Fannie will never get married." *Mamm* spoke so loudly that Fannie knew *Mammi* must surely have been out gathering eggs in the henhouse. "Over thirty and not a man in the community willing to take her on."

Fannie sighed and continued down the stairs. Would they never give up? If her *mamm* only knew how much she longed for a family of her own. "But it must not be in God's plan, so let it be," she whispered to herself.

She descended a few more steps and could clearly see the hubbub of activity in the kitchen. Her *mamm*, Verna Hochstetler, moved from table to stove to countertop, dropping vegetables into the soup she was making for lunch and at the same time tending a sizzling frying pan on the stove.

She'd been right about her *mammi* being outside.

Now her grandmother was trying to get through the backdoor while balancing a basket of eggs. The door slammed behind her with a bang.

Mamm stirred the pot of boiling soup, and steam floated upward, swirling to the ceiling, spreading throughout the kitchen and beyond. The scent of onion along with other spices made Fannie's stomach growl. No time like the present to make her entrance.

She let her boots tap out an extra loud thump to give *Mamm* and *Mammi* a warning that she was coming. Neither woman paid any attention. Their chatter covered any sounds Fannie made descending the stairs.

Mammi Frieda waddled to the kitchen table. "Let the girl alone, for Pete's sake. She'll settle down in good time."

Her *mamm* frowned. She put a fist on her hip and leaned against the cabinet. "You're awful sure about Fannie. She's as tough as beef jerky on a winter day. I'd like to see the man who takes her hand."

Frieda grunted. "You will see him, I have no doubt. After all, my son married you, didn't he, speaking of tough and opinionated women?"

At that comment, Fannie hurried into the kitchen before the fireworks started.

Why wouldn't *Mamm* and *Mammi* consider she might be able to hear them? Although she shouldn't be surprised. Even if they did know, they likely wouldn't hold back their thoughts.

"Good morning," she said, smiling in an attempt to break the tension. They scowled in return. "Who's so opinionated?" she teased, knowing the answer before it left her *mammi*'s lips.

"You are strong headed. Don't try to say anything

different. You're just like your *mamm*." Frieda pushed up her nose when she took a big whiff of the bubbling soup. "Too many onions."

Fannie knew what would come next. A lengthy conversation on how much onion was enough, according to *Mamm*, and what was too much, according to *Mammi*.

"Clears your chest," one often said and then the conversation would continue on to another monumental issue that needed to be discussed, argued about, and not resolved.

Gazing out the large kitchen window, Fannie scanned the horizon. *Mamm* and *Mammi* were off on the onion debate. At least they'd lost interest in her marriage prospects. Or rather, lack thereof.

Fields of tilled earth as far as she could see were dotted with white houses, hay barns, silos, and cows. What else was out there? She'd read about mountains that scraped the sky, beaches that welcomed the tide, and trees so old they were seedlings when Christ walked the earth.

Fannie leaned forward and tucked her hand under her chin, knowing there was more past the barn than she could imagine, and she had a pretty good imagination.

Thoughts of leaving her community swirled in her mind like fog over the pasture, but then slowly dissipated. She was expected to court James Miller—younger than her, but about as stiff-necked as she was. Which explained why no commitment would be made.

She was just too independent to need a man in her life. At least that's what she liked to believe.

"What are you daydreaming about?" Frieda was a

bossy woman, but Fannie had to admit she kept things in order. "We have lots to do today."

"*Jah*, I'll see how much milk there is compared to yesterday. We need some nice green grass to keep up our dairy farming side of things," Fannie said.

On her way to the milk barn she noticed a truck trundling down the lane, a cat's tail of dust curling behind it. As soon as she was sure who it was, her stomach stirred a little. Spring in the Amish community meant several things: new babes for one and regular visits from Daniel for another.

She tucked a wisp of hair into her *kapp* and went back in to wash her face. She returned to the mudroom just before Dr. Daniel Kauffman stepped inside behind her.

"Morning, Fannie." He pulled off his boots and put them next to hers.

"After you." He motioned to her and kept a close distance as they walked into the white kitchen, with the smell of bacon filling their nostrils.

He seemed to have put aside his usual sharp mannerisms, which always caused her to put up her guard. "What brings you here?"

It was a common question whenever he was in the community. His presence usually meant someone needed extra care or Doc Reuben wasn't available for a birth.

He ignored her question and greeted the busy women cooking up a delicious breakfast.

They would give him little choice as to whether or not he was hungry, but she knew he would eat lightly. He was always on call, if only in his mind. A heavy meal meant a tired doctor.

"Just coffee and toast, Frieda. I have a delivery coming to the hospital soon. My time is short."

He took a sip of the coffee and then another. "This reminds me of the coffee I drank when I was overseas. I wish they had this at the hospital."

Fannie lifted her brows in surprise. "You went overseas? I didn't know that."

"I took a semester off between college and medical school." He sipped again. "Nothing takes me back there like a cup of good strong coffee."

"I'll never tell you what the secret is or you won't come back." Frieda handed him a slice of homemade bread with a dollop of strawberry jam nestled next to it. He didn't decline it, but he ate only the toast, Fannie noticed.

"I'm here to see Fannie." He wiped his mouth and dropped the napkin on the table.

Fannie jolted at the sound of her name. "About what?"

Verna gave Fannie a warning frown.

He regarded her a moment, his brown eyes piercing hers. "My practice at the hospital has grown, and my patients here are in need. I've decided to split my time between the two."

"What does that have to do with me?"

"You're the best midwife in the community." He took a bite of toast.

"Pshaw." She scoffed. "I don't even have my license yet."

"Even so, you're in demand." Verna muttered behind her. She'd obviously been listening as she cooked. "Isn't that so, Fannie?"

Daniel sipped his coffee, seeming to stifle a smile.

"I'm sure Fannie is capable. I need someone in the community at the clinic to help me with occasional deliveries. I can supervise while you acquire your needed hours for the license."

Irritation creased Fannie's forehead. Between Daniel and her *mamm*, her future was decided. She stood taller, straightened her shoulders, and set her jaw firmly into place. She couldn't imagine working with Daniel. They were just too much alike. Both stubborn as mules. They'd bickered and scolded each other since he'd arrived in the community to help old Doc Reuben.

"We need to talk." She looked at him evenly, and then headed outside while he lagged behind for some unknown reason. Probably to say good-bye to her *mamm* and *mammi*. Heaven only knew why.

She leaned against his truck and waited, tapping her booted foot.

He worked his jaw when he finally stepped out of the *haus* and approached her. "Just what do you take me for, putting me on the spot like that?" she demanded, stepping closer before he could answer. "I'm not here to do your bidding, you know."

He ran a hand through his short brown hair and regarded her. "This is your community, not mine anymore. If you want your people to get the medical assistance they need, you'll help me make this happen."

"You dismissed yourself of us too easily. Do you think this will make us accept you after the way you shunned us and our ways?"

His jaw tightened again, but after he drew in a deep breath and swallowed, he seemed calm. "You'll accompany me on rounds for a week or two, help with deliveries, then start seeing women at the clinic in town." He climbed into his truck. "You might want to talk to the elders before you make assumptions. They told me to ask you. And I have not shunned you or the community."

"You didn't ask," she said to as he cranked the engine. "You commanded."

The motor coughed as he drove away, leaving a cloud of exhaust behind. She covered her face, wiping it with her apron.

She watched him go, her irritation growing. Then she spun on one heel and headed to the barn, wondering why this and why her? Was he really that desperate or was there another reason for him to involve her? If something was going on, she needed to find out—and not from him.

As she stepped inside the milk barn, the swishing sounds of a handheld milking machine greeted her. Her *mamm* sat on a stool behind the milk cow. "Why did Daniel leave so quickly?"

Something in her *mamm*'s expression said something was sure enough brewing, and it didn't involve milking cows.

"Need some help?" Her *mamm*'s offer was casual enough, but Fannie knew she wanted to talk. Her goal in life was for her daughters to become brides, even though Verna made it clear she believed marriage might not be in Fannie's future and that she was disturbed over the notion.

"*Nee*, you forget that I do most of the milking." Fannie headed over to the white and black Guernsey milk cow with her sisters who were doing more playing than milking.

Her *mamm* stepped aside, wiping her hands on her apron. "So what do you think of Daniel's offer?" *Mamm* asked, wasting no time getting to her point.

"That he's manipulative and controlling. But when he puts it in terms of what's right for the community, he gives me no option." Fannie huffed a sigh of exasperation at the same time the cow slapped her with her tail.

Mamm was unusually quiet for a moment. "Option for what?"

"Being his assistant at births." She kept her eyes on the cow's udder instead of her *mamm*.

"I would think it a compliment," her *mamm* said. "Choosing you shows how much he thinks of you."

Fannie snorted. "I doubt that. And I don't want to be 'chosen' by anyone."

"I don't know why you're being stubborn about it, especially when you have such a passion for helping others in need. Isn't that why you want to be a licensed midwife?" She chuckled lightly. "Besides, what about that old horse of ours. Didn't you want to save up to buy a new one?"

"I didn't think you favored using my working money to buy Ap."

Mamm's head snapped up. "*Ach*, no." *Mamm* knew once Fannie gave an animal a name, it was a keeper. This was one of those times. "We need a horse. But you're going to have to expect some questions if you have an Appaloosa running around the community. Those spotted coats draw so much attention."

"It's been done. Remember the Fischers' horse?"

"*Jah*, but that was a different situation. Abby Fischer was new to our ways. You are not." *Mamm* lifted a brow, her way of saying she was right and the matter should be settled. “She wasn’t even aware of the Amish ways until she married into our community.”

“It’s for me to decide.” As soon as the words were out, Fannie realized she should have kept quiet. Her *mamm*’s eyes lifted, Fannie’s sign to be wary.

“Anyway, it’s not likely I’d make much money working with Daniel. You know how it is. Doc Reuben usually gets paid with pies and chickens.” Fannie chuckled at the thought then fell quiet.

Her *mamm* didn’t have to point out the reasons to take Daniel up on his offer. She wanted to be a midwife. She wanted to bring new life into the world. She couldn’t imagine such joy. Working with him would give her the hours she needed for her license. Almost as much as that, she wanted to buy that beautiful, dancing Appaloosa. But no matter the passion she felt for achieving both goals, she would have to spend time with Daniel. She let out another irritated sigh before turning back to the *haus*.

What had she gotten herself into?

Chapter Two

The next day, when Daniel stopped by to pick up Fannie, Doc Reuben was sitting in a rocking chair on the porch of her house, rocking slowly and seemingly enjoying the serenity of the pastoral scene.

Daniel figured there had to be a better reason than watching the sunrise over the pasture for Doc to have planted himself on Fannie's front porch.

It was no secret in the community that Daniel and Fannie had a reputation for spats, large and small, and had acted that way toward each other since they'd met.

Maybe Doc figured he'd better oversee their new venture. Or maybe Fannie's mother and grandmother enlisted him to see things off to a smooth start.

Doc looked up and smiled as Daniel strode closer. "*Danke* for taking the time to help us out," he said as Daniel pulled up a chair beside him. "As I mentioned the other day, we are being blessed with a great number of expected deliveries this spring and, from what I hear, an even greater number than we originally thought." His grin widened as he focused on the barn in the distance.

Daniel turned to follow the old doctor's gaze. Fannie

had just come out of the barn and was headed toward the house, her red hair gleaming in the early morning sunlight.

"I heard the *gut* news," Doc said. "It seems you took my advice and got yourself an assistant."

"Not yet. She's going to ride along with me today and then decide. So she says." He rolled his eyes and sighed while watching Fannie walk toward them. He admired the confident way she carried herself, her chin tilted upward, her shoulders straight and strong. He'd seen her hold her own, doing whatever struck her fancy. And she seemed to do as well or better than most men he knew. But, of course, he'd never tell her.

"Are you ready?" She turned toward the truck without so much as a "good morning" tossed his way.

What a pain.

He practically leapt off the porch to catch up with her to take the lead, but she kept ahead of him by at least three strides. He could hear Doc chuckling as they got into the truck.

She seemed steamed, really steamed that she had to be here with him, no matter the mission they were on. No matter that he'd asked her to simply ride along and observe. He'd heard throughout the community about her passion for bringing babies into the world and the easy way she had with mothers. But there was obviously something stuck in her craw. He sighed, knowing what that something was—being with him.

If only Fannie knew he had little choice in the matter. She was the best midwife, therefore the best choice, to help him with the overabundance of deliveries that would soon be coming. She would also be an ideal helper for him with the overflow of clients in the community. But if she ever found out how reluctant he was to hire her, there would be heck to pay.

Not to mention he'd have to find someone else to assist him, and that was not something he wanted to consider. He'd seen Fannie in action, and she'd done well. With all the babies in an Amish community due in the spring, he needed more help, plain and simple. The hospital was generous in allowing him to use some of his hours in the community, but he couldn't be there full-time.

Truth be told, someone easier to get along with would make things better. But he couldn't opt for his personal choice versus doing what was right for the patients. And Fannie was the best. No doubt about it. So in the end, this wasn't about him; it was about getting the best person for the job for the good of the community.

Fannie broke into his thoughts. "So, where are we headed first?"

"I want to acquaint you with those on my rounds. Right now we're headed to see the Keims." He glanced across at her. "Do you know them?"

Fannie nodded.

"All you need to do today is observe. I'll tell you if there's anything more you'll need to do."

"Or not," she said. He thought he saw a hint of a smile as she stared straight ahead. They rode in silence the rest of the way.

As he parked his pickup, Daniel heard a sound—a cry or whimper—coming from the house.

He hurried from the pickup with Fannie right behind him.

An older man hit the other side of the screen door and bolted out of the house. He paused when he saw Daniel and leaned over, wheezing.

"Thank *Gott*, you're here." He wiped his forehead with a hanky and stood, still breathing hard, his face pale. "Go on in. I'll be back once I catch my breath."

A stab of worry hit Daniel. The man's stress level was over the top. He glanced at Fannie and could see from her expression that she was as concerned as he was. She nodded for Daniel to go on in; she would take care of the father-to-be.

Seconds later Daniel took the stairs two at a time. By the time he made it to the second level, the woman's cries had grown louder. He followed the sound to the doorway of a small bedroom. There before him was a woman doubled over her large stomach. By her side was an older woman whom he recognized—Ruth Miller, his patient's mother.

Other women hovered nearby. Relatives and friends, he supposed. As he hurried to her beside, he remembered the family. Mrs. Miller's husband, Mark, was the man in full-stress mode downstairs with Fannie, and his patient was their daughter, Esther.

"Mind if I take a look?" Daniel reached for Esther's hand.

She gripped his hand and squeezed.

"This one's giving her fits." Mrs. Miller shook her head. "Glad you came when you did. I've run out of energy. "

"Is this her first?" He'd just started to clean his hands when another shrill cry erupted from Esther. He hurried through the process with a disinfectant then rinsed them in a bowl of water.

"Number ten. Unless it's another set of twins." She covered her cough with a bony hand and dropped it. "The others are at the neighbor's so the *haus* would be quiet."

After working in the city, Daniel had greater appreciation for the stamina of Amish women. Most of the time they delivered with little or no help at all. Baby number ten would likely arrive quite soon.

"This was just supposed to be a routine checkup. I'm glad we came here first."

"*Jah*," Mrs. Miller said. The other women nodded in agreement. "And it's a good thing those cars go fast, I guess."

He bit back a smile. Most Amish wouldn't even step inside a car, let alone ride in one. Their generation seemed to still follow all the rules involving the Amish ways.

Mrs. Miller prattled on as he examined Esther. He had learned how to multitask. Like today, there were usually a few family members around. The men stayed downstairs, and the women helped upstairs.

Daniel needed more warm water and clean towels and thought of Fannie downstairs, taking care of the wheezing older man. Though she had agreed to ride along to make her decision, she'd seen the grandfather-to-be and jumped in to help. He couldn't help but admire her spirit.

Within a few minutes Daniel heard a prairie warbler's distinctive and tremulous whistle outside the window just as the baby made his way into the world. A nice touch. He couldn't have asked for a better herald of a new life being born. A sudden stirring in his heart surprised him: he wished someone could have shared the moment with him. The birdsong. The babe's wee cry. Even more surprising, the someone who flashed into his mind's eye was Fannie.

He washed his hands again with disinfectant and as he dried them, smiled at the new mother.

"Congratulations, you have a boy." He didn't say the baby was healthy until he knew that clinically, which could be touchy at times. He wasn't one to make idle promises.

Mrs. Miller reached for the baby, which made Daniel a little nervous considering how exhausted she appeared. "Have either of you gotten much sleep?"

Both she and the new mother shook their heads. "Not since I lost my water," Esther said with a little laugh. "I've been through this often enough to know it was no time for anyone to be sleeping."

"And you won't be getting much now with this fine little one." The grandmother held the babe as if he were the first child ever to be born on earth.

An aunt sat down next to her and took a turn holding the new little one and so it went. Daniel smiled. He had never seen a neglected new Amish baby.

"*Danke*, Doc. I felt better with you helping. You know how the community doctor is here," Mrs. Miller said.

"And this is still his place. I'm just helping out for a while."

"It's *gut* there are more than one of you around to help, what with the number of deliveries you'll have," Esther said.

"No doubt about that." He picked up his stethoscope and forceps and dropped them into the disinfectant. No nurse or aide here to do this task, unlike at the hospital. He was doctor, nurse, and aide all rolled into one.

Mrs. Miller finally took her eyes off the baby to look at him. "We were all very sorry to hear about your wife, Daniel."

He gulped. "Thank you. It's been a long…I'm fine, but thank you."

She nodded once. "Does this mean you'll be staying with us for a while?"

"Yes, though I need help…" He again thought of Fannie downstairs, irritated she hadn't at least checked in with him. "I don't usually do the tasks a nurse does anymore."

The room fell silent.

What had he said? He cast his mind back to his Amish days, to think what would cause the pause.

Ruth Miller handed the baby over to his *mamm*. "Well then, I'll gather these for you." She bustled about, scooped up Daniel's instruments, and dropped them with the others into the disinfectant. "

He raised a hand. "That's not what I was fishing for, but I appreciate the offer." Although he preferred not doing the menial tasks, he realized he might have been a bit presumptuous.

"*Nee*, *mamm* and baby need to spend time together." She brought over a bowl of water someone had earlier prepared for sponging the baby. She lifted the babe from his mother's arms and bathed him, cooing as she did. Daniel dried and packed his utensils without delay.

"Well, ladies, I'll be off." He latched his bag shut.

"*Nee*, let me fix you a snack to go," one of the ladies said, "and some goat's milk."

He held up a hand again, maybe too quickly this time, but he'd never found anything involving goat appealing. However, when he saw the ladies' expressions, he decided not to protest. "Don't mind if I do."

The *mammi* hurried to the kitchen and returned with a bag she thrust at him. Even before he saw what was stuffed in his bag, he knew it had no room for even another crumb of zucchini bread.

"It's the least we can do. *Danke*, Doctor."

He reached for his satchel and headed for the door. "Ladies, good day."

"I'll walk you out." The *mammi* twisted her apron in one hand.

That wasn't usually a good sign, if they couldn't speak around family. Fannie came up, and he gave her a silent sign to give him time alone with Mrs. Miller. Fannie instinctively understood and stayed inside.

"What can I help you with?" he asked Mrs. Miller as they walked away from the house.

She stood directly in front of him and wrung her hands. "I didn't want to say anything, but it keeps getting worse." She peeked around him toward the front door.

Daniel frowned. "What is getting worse?"

"Her husband." That seemed to be all she thought she needed to say.

He had been gone long enough to know better than to guess. "I remember him, but I haven't seen him in a long while." He let her continue, but he closed his eyes at the thought of being more involved than simply delivering the occasional baby. Though given his strange status—of the community, yet not—he knew better than to think these sort of situations wouldn't happen. He just wasn't ready to confront it, not so soon.

"He's had a tough time making ends meet. Had a bad crop and has been impossible to live with. Would you give him a good word when you see him? Maybe even come for dinner." She was so hopeful, how could he say no? Yet he didn't want to let folks think this could lead to something bigger. Working at two places so far apart was too much already.

"I don't know how I can help and I'm very busy this time of—"

"*Jah*, I know. Sorry to bother. *Danke* for coming to help with the delivery. You have a gift, ya know. Bless you." With that she smiled and walked down the dirt path, presumably to the neighboring farm where the other nine siblings waited to hear about the newest addition to the family.

Daniel continued to watch her and told himself to move forward to the next stop. There was no time to waste. Fannie must have been watching from a window. She hurried to catch up with him as he made his way to the pickup.

She strode next to him as they passed by the crop Mrs. Miller mentioned.

"That doesn't look good," Fannie said. "Not a healthy crop at all."

He nodded, but didn't tell her what Mrs. Miller had said. After all, it wasn't any of his business. He needed to keep moving.

A few minutes after being on their way, Daniel spotted the new *daed*, Esther's husband, Judah, walking down the back forty with his hands on his hips.

He bowed his head, and Daniel didn't know if he was just lowering his head or bowing to pray. Because Daniel wasn't in a good way with the Almighty, maybe this would be a time to do a good deed for one of God's chosen.

Daniel took pity on the man, turned onto a spot near the dusty fallow field, and parked. He knew what it was like to be in a bad way when life wasn't so good. He told Fannie to stay in the pickup as he got out.

"*Hallo.*" The German word came back to him easily even though he hadn't spoken it for longer than he could recall.

When the man lifted his head, Daniel remembered him, and not in a good way. He was one who didn't share the idea of Daniel leaving with a blessing. Most didn't, but this particular man wasn't one who treated many in the same way he wanted to be treated. Judah was a difficult man in the best of circumstances. Maybe, though, because he was a new father, this was a good day for him.

Daniel contemplated if he should keep walking or pause and speak some encouraging words to this man. As he drew closer, he saw the man had a gun. A rifle.

He quickened his pace then turned his walk into a run. Just as he did, the man dropped the rifle to his side.

Daniel took a deep breath and tried to compose himself. "You doing some hunting or planting?"

The man's bloodshot eyes said everything along with the slumped shoulders and wary disposition. "Well, if it isn't Dr. Kauffman." He wiped his nose but didn't look away. "Somebody come down with something?"

"Not that I know of. Why? You feeling ill?" Best to

play dumb rather than ask too many questions. That was the surest way to lose the conversation.

He scoffed. "I guess you could say that." He slapped his cheek then flicked away a mosquito.

"Esther had the baby." Daniel watched his face for any twitch or smile or indication of pride or happiness.

The man just grunted.

They were quiet for a moment; Daniel didn't want to irritate him and hoped to coax him to talk.

"This crop just took away my family's food come fall." His chest moved more rapidly the more he spoke. "You have a family, Doc?"

He shook his head. "No, you're fortunate."

He pursed his lips and scanned the field again. "Guess I'll go home and see about the wife."

"Yes, you should do that."

They both took a minute and then each went the opposite way. As Daniel got into his truck, a strange loneliness overtook him.

Fannie's expression said she understood, and she lifted her hand slightly as if she wanted to pat his. But instead, she just fixed her green-eyed gaze on him and remained silent.

Chapter Three

Fannie woke to the bright morning light. She must have slept in, unusual for her. Her thoughts as she went to bed had kept her awake until nearly dawn.

The prospect of spending more time with Daniel and helping at the clinic flustered her. Yesterday he'd treated her with such detachment. She knew she irritated him, but he also was brusque and hard to get along with.

Thank the Lord the daylight had brought her a new perspective. She loved to help others, and she wasn't about to let Daniel or anyone else interfere with that passion.

The door creaked, opening just enough for her *mammi* to peek in. "Are you awake?"

A pointless question, Fannie thought. "What time is it?" She glanced toward the streaming sunlight coming through her window.

"What's causing you to lie abed?" *Mammi* entered her room and stood with her arms crossed. "You're usually the first one up."

Her pause should have prepared Fannie for what was to come, but she realized it too late. *Mamm* walked in.

"Someone is here for you." *Mamm* kept her voice even, holding in her obvious irritation. "Since you have a visitor, you might want to dress up a bit." She lifted one brow. "Don't waste your time up here. He's in a hurry, as usual." The door shut without any opportunity to question his reasons for the visit.

"We'll talk later." *Mammi* winked and started for the door.

"*Nee*, they can wait." Fannie planted her feet on the cold wood floor and stood. "What's on your mind?"

Mammi grimaced but managed to ask her question. "What would you do if a woman came to you with child?"

"Married?" Fannie stared as she asked.

"*Nee*."

"And the baby?" She never even blinked.

"Healthy. What if it wasn't?"

"What kinds of questions are these?" Fannie asked. It was difficult to be irritated with *Mammi*, but in this case Fannie was quickly losing patience.

"They are some of the questions I'll be asked if you work at an English hospital." *Mammi*'s gaze was open and guileless.

Fannie took long strides to her closet and dressed. "Could you do it?"

"*Nee*, not nursing work. But possibly a bedside sprinkle of encouragement." She smiled, taking in the words she'd just spoken. "Mmm, *jah*, that sounds about right."

"For you. I've been told I don't have a sweet bedside manner." Fannie twisted her red hair up and fastened it in place. She hoped *Mammi* would deny it, but wasn't surprised that she didn't.

"*Ach*, you have other qualities that are more important. You get things done. And you're quick to catch on." She nodded. "The question is, do you want to do this?"

"That's what I've been asking myself."

"I have no doubt of your abilities."

"My doubts aren't about the job but about working with him." She adjusted her *kapp* on her head, then tucked a few wayward strands of hair under it. "But the job is working here in the community, not in the hospital. This I can do."

Mammi chuckled. "Well, you are confident. I'll give you that much."

"All right then, it's decided." Fannie put her hands on her hips and held her head up high as she made her way to the stairs. "Are you coming?'

Mammi caught up and followed her to the kitchen where Daniel sat at the large table. Fannie pulled out a chair.

"Morning." Daniel lifted one side of his mouth and directed his attention to Fannie. His brown eyes grew warm, almost affectionate. No, she must have imagined it, because now he looked the same as ever, businesslike and detached.

"I've decided to take the job."

He nodded and waited, as if he knew she had more to say. "I figured as much."

She lifted an eyebrow. "Well then, don't be so assuming in the future. And remember who I'm doing this for."

"We're both doing this for the same reason. I remember where my roots are. You don't need to tell me what's most important here."

They were silent for a minute too long, and he finally stood. "I don't want to start out on the wrong foot. I want to help the people here and you want the same."

She'd always hated it when people assumed what she was thinking or saying—especially when the person was right. They left the *haus* and headed to his truck.

Inside the pickup Fannie turned to Daniel, her brow wrinkled with concern. "Daniel, I don't just want to be your assistant. I want to learn what you're doing. Can you teach me?"

"I have to keep my eyes on the patient. You're secondary." He rubbed his forehead. "What I mean is, I'll get the job done in less time if I do it myself without taking time to explain every little thing to you." He started the truck and they headed down the lane.

The last thing Fannie wanted was to hear him constantly barking orders. "There are things people do to train others with their knowledge. You learned from someone at one time."

He lifted his head. "Yes, but by the time I arrive, many of the mothers don't have much time left or the baby is in distress. We have to work quickly. I won't always be able to explain everything I'm doing. Oftentimes a good outcome is dependent on quick action."

"All right, I understand." She looked him in the eye. "But it doesn't mean I like it. You'll teach me when you can, though? In return I will not pester you with questions during an emergency."

He nodded.

She felt his gaze on her and wondered what he was thinking.

"We have a couple of stops. This family is not familiar

to me, Luke and Neva?" He frowned as he turned off the road and down a lane bordered by healthy looking oak trees.

He usually remembered every patient, from the hospital to the farm, as well as every problem. It was enough to make her head spin.

"You'll probably remember them when we get there. Luke at least. Neva had trouble conceiving and feeling a part of the family. I'm sure the new baby is a blessing. Neva's very shy."

"Then you're the right person to help assess her condition."

"I think she may have the baby blues, but only time will tell. Like as not, she isn't having people in the *haus*."

"Somewhat phobic." He said it more to himself.

Fannie could learn a lot just listening to his insight. She could do this, she told herself. She could work with this man who made her stomach feel so odd.

As soon as they got out of the truck, Luke jogged over. He was a handsome and caring man, a good match for Neva. As soon as Daniel shut the truck door Luke stood solidly in front of them as if to block them from the *haus*.

"*Hallo*, Doc. Fannie."

"Good to see you, Luke," Fannie said. "I'm looking forward to seeing your lovely wife and the new babe." Fannie hoped the hint let him know their intentions. There were times she felt Neva wanted her to leave before Fannie could get out of her buggy.

"Let's hope so. Come on in." His long legs kept Fannie in a slow run to stay beside him.

The screen door creaked as they walked into the mudroom, and Fannie was nearly overcome by an odd pungent smell. The *haus* was a mess. Piles of clothes and spoiled food sat in the kitchen sink.

Daniel took one look and hurried up the stairs to his patient.

Luke looked over at her and let out a breath. "Sorry the place is a mess. But you came here for Neva and the babe."

"And for you." She picked up a sour-smelling dishrag. "The doctor will call if he needs me." Luke's bloodshot eyes said he was beyond exhaustion. "How's the babe?"

He frowned. "You'll have to tell me."

"You can't take care of the baby if you don't take care of yourself." Fannie rinsed and stacked the dishes and then heated water as she talked. It helped twofold. She was getting work done, and Daniel had time alone with the patient.

"Do you mind, Luke?" While she waited for the water to boil, she hurried over to a basket of clothes, separated the clean from dirty, then folded a few clean shirts. When the water was nearing a boil, she added soap and started washing the dishes.

He shook his head but remained mute.

Daniel came down the stairs and nodded to Fannie to go check on Neva. As she climbed the stairs, she heard snatches of the conversation between Daniel and Luke —"tired," "blood loss," and "bed rest."

"How are *mamm* and child this morning?" Fannie sat on the bed beside them and stroked the little one's head lightly.

"You didn't need to come, Fannie. I'm grateful you did, but I hate to bother you both." Neva looked wan, her face nearly matching the white pillowcase she rested against.

"Dr. Kauffman sounded positive, didn't he?" Her words seemed hopeful even though nothing was sure unless he could make an assessment through the hospital.

"I don't know what's wrong with me." Then the tears came, and Fannie didn't know what to say.

"He's a good doctor." She could honestly say that without hesitation, and perhaps it gave some encouragement.

Neva smiled slightly and brushed the little one's blond hair away so Fannie could see him better. He appeared fine by looking at him, though his breathing sounded a bit raspy.

"And you're well, Neva?"

"*Jah*, just tired."

"I'll be back to bring a casserole for you, if you like." It would be a relief for Luke and nutrition for Neva. And that meant the baby would breastfeed well.

Neva took her hand. "Thanks for coming, Fannie. Don't worry about fixing food. We're fine."

Fannie squeezed her hand and left. She found Daniel walking to the door with Luke. They stopped when they saw her descending the stairs.

"Has she been eating well, Luke?" Fannie asked when she reached them.

He shrugged. "About the same as usual."

"I'd like to bring you dinner."

He nodded then looked up to Neva's room obviously worried his wife might not accept such help.

"I'm making a casserole for the family so one more won't be any trouble."

"Neva is a bit standoffish when it comes to accepting help. She'll want to know how she can repay you—if she agrees to your offer at all."

"Then we won't give her a chance to refuse," Fannie said gently. "Someday when someone else needs some help, she can fix them a casserole. It's the way we take care of each other. I'll see you around dinnertime then."

"All right, then." Daniel nodded and gave her the shadow of a smile as they got into his pickup. "Something's eating at you. What is it?"

She didn't return the smile. "You know, there's more to helping out a neighbor than just tending to their medical needs."

He stared at her as he started the engine. "What makes you think I don't care about their other needs?"

"Just now. Your face was a storm cloud when you saw me working in the kitchen. I suppose you think my efforts were wasted cleaning dishes rather than helping you out. And when we visited the Keims yesterday, and you talked with Judah Keim out in his field…he was holding a rifle, and it wasn't for hunting. Did it occur to you that the man was at the end of his rope? That you might be able to reach out to him and help?" She shook her head slowly. "And to think, his wife just had their tenth child." She felt the heat of tears and turned to look out the window so Daniel wouldn't see them.

They left the community and drove down the one-lane highway, then Daniel took a turn off the road without saying a word.

"Where are we going?"

He grunted and his face tightened. "It's just a visit I

have to make. I wouldn't be bringing you if I had time to come back."

"Back where?" She was confused and frustrated he didn't make himself plain.

"I have to check on someone." His voice held a certain irritation, telling her to let it go. But letting anything go had never been easy for her. She was far more likely to hang on like a cranky dog and his bone.

She bit her lip to keep from saying something she shouldn't and then for the hundredth time considered that working with him might have been her worst decision ever. She was strong-willed, but he was worse, if such a thing were possible.

They drove up to an old farm that had seen better days. Acres of land with only a scattering of dirt stretched as far as the eye could see. No crop could possibly be planted without a complete work over. Plowing and fertilizer would be first up.

Dust blew, creating small whirlwinds and a couple larger ones. She closed her eyes until her cheeks hurt with the effort.

Daniel parked the truck. "Stay here," he said as he climbed out.

She scrambled out of the passenger side and hurried to catch up to him. No one was going to tell her what to do.

He walked to the nearest shelter, a worn-down porch with not a bit of color, just wooden boards that seemed to never have had any paint.

"Do you treat this family?" The place looked abandoned.

He ignored her and took slow steps toward the front

door. "I thought I told you to stay in the pickup." His jaw tightened.

She drew in a deep breath, ready with a quick, ornery comeback, but something in his expression stopped her. He let out a loud sigh when she kept walking with him. Finally he turned. "Stay here," he growled and then, turning again to the door, he headed inside, closing it behind him.

Within seconds loud voices echoed from inside. The words were muffled, so she inched closer.

She stepped back quickly when she heard Daniel's boots hitting the hollow wood floors as he headed to the door. Her cheeks were warm as she hurried to the porch steps. Daniel stormed through the door just as her dress caught on a nail on the worn out railing. Without a word, Daniel grabbed her arm and propelled her to the truck.

The whole thing happened so quickly she wasn't sure what to ask first. She finally had to say something. "No one deserves to be shouted at the way you shouted at that patient."

When she glanced over at him, she saw a vein in his neck throbbing and decided to keep silent.

Now was not the time for questions.

Chapter Four

Jack Johnson's BMW was parked on the street in front of Daniel's house when he swung into his driveway. He hit the remote for the garage door, drove in, and parked next to his Mercedes.

His friend got out of the BMW, closed the door, and headed up the drive. But Daniel was in no mood to talk, not with Fannie, not with Jack, not with anyone—especially after the falling out with his dad at the house on the hill. But it was Friday night. And Friday night dinner was their routine. Ordinarily Daniel looked as forward as Jack did to a relaxing evening after a long week at the hospital.

Tonight was different. The idea of making small talk irked him. And he knew from experience that rehashing why he was spending so much time with the Amish would fall on deaf ears

Jack grinned as he approached. "We still on for tonight?" He turned his wrist to look at the time.

"Go on and I'll catch up." He was busier during the spring, but then Jack already knew that. They had gone through residency together and had each other's backs all through the long shifts. Jack knew about Daniel's Amish upbringing but rarely mentioned it.

"You're not trying to get out of this?" Jack lifted his brow. At times Daniel thought Jack knew him better than he knew himself. "Come on, you need to relax. Get out, have some fun." He pointed to his watch. "We can still hit happy hour."

"I need to change. I'll meet you there."

"I'll wait. Gotta make a call."

Daniel hoped it was a call in to the hospital but knew how selfish that was. For the most part he enjoyed Jack's friendship, but he was sometimes uncomfortable with his behavior.

He showered and got dressed—khakis, a light blue shirt, and a darker blue sweater. It struck him as frivolous compared to the black suit he wore in the community. His mind traveled through the day he'd spent with Fannie. They were defensive and cranky with each other when they were alone, but got along better when they worked together. There was something endearing about her but also something exasperating. Then he paused for one second and wondered if she felt the same about him.

"You ready?" Jack called from the front door. He was always antsy, a trait that often made Daniel nervous during surgery. Daniel was glad he didn't work with him anymore, even though Jack had an impeccable record.

Daniel headed into the living room where Jack waited. He scooped up his keys wondering if this was going to be another sit-down that left him wondering if he'd ever meet someone special. Their Friday nights out were usually the same every time. They'd only meet women looking for a relationship for all the wrong reasons.

Jack jingled his keys. "I'll drive. You've just done a double shift. Besides I'm parked out front."

"Nah, I'm all right. I'm not planning on staying late."

"Aren't you going to have any fun tonight?" Jack scoffed.

"Sorry, a man's got to do what a man's got to do. For me that means an early night." Daniel was no pushover, and Jack knew it, which made Daniel wonder if he had something up his sleeve.

"What do you have in mind?"

"Who? Me? Nothing." He shrugged.

Daniel was becoming less interested in going out on the weekends, especially if he was on call at the hospital.

Daniel enjoyed the Mercedes's comfortable ride but appreciated the safety of the car even more. He hadn't grown up with this kind of luxury, and the drive felt good after a long day in that rattletrap truck bumping down rutted lanes.

He swerved onto the highway and caught up with Jack's BMW. They jockeyed for position, but Daniel played it safe. They were settled in with only a few miles to their destination when Daniel's left hand began to tremble.

A car zoomed by. The exhaust alone was enough to disorient him but when the car weaved between him and Jack, Daniel panicked and roared to the closest exit.

Anxiety flowed through him as he tried to put the pieces together. A trembling hand. A crazy driver. Late for dinner. He pulled to the curb and watched his hand quiver.

Jack parked behind him and approached the driver's side window. "You all right?"

"I'm fine. Stupid traffic. My hand started shaking."

"Crazy driver. We're almost there."

He couldn't find the words to explain what happened. He wanted nothing more than to turn around, go home, and go to bed. But Jack would never hear of it.

"I'll take it slower." He held his wrist, trying to decipher if what happened was related to the anxiety that was now subsiding.

Daniel spent the rest of the drive putting the pieces together. A hand tremor could indicate too many things for him to narrow down. Jack's lack of concern somehow made him feel better.

As soon as they got to the restaurant, Jack headed to the bar while Daniel made his way to a corner booth. He stared at his hand. Whatever had caused the tremor had passed. He thought about what he would say to a patient. One incident wasn't enough to worry about it. Tomorrow would be another day of deliveries and then the night shift at the hospital.

Jack came over with drinks. Soda for them both. Jack was on the night shift this week so he had to eat and drink carefully.

"I'm glad this week is over. You okay?" Daniel reached for his cola.

"I am. I could eat though. How about you?"

"Starving." He waved the waitress over and they ordered.

"How much longer are you going to work for the Amish?" Jack's tone grated on Daniel. There were babies born outside the Amish community as well.

"As long as it takes."

"Your one-liners don't work for me." Jack sipped his drink and watched Daniel over the rim of the glass.

"I know you don't agree with what I'm doing for the Amish."

"You don't live with them anymore. So what's the point? They call you when they need you and—"

"We buy their food, and they work for us when we want handiwork done, among other things. Sounds like a good deal all around." Daniel really didn't want this conversation to continue, but it wasn't something that was going to change. The Amish were commonly misunderstood.

Their food arrived, and they continued the conversation as they ate.

"Sounds like a boring life to me." Jack dug into his steak.

"It was a good place to grow up."

"Then why did you leave?" Jack had asked some idle questions occasionally but hadn't seemed too interested in the answers.

"I wanted to be a doctor. The Amish can't go to school after they get to a certain age."

"I heard something about that. Seems harsh."

"To each his own." Daniel shrugged. Enough explaining. He'd heard the tourists asking about the Amish like they were movie stars and yet they'd complain about their ways at the same time. "You about ready to go?"

Jack frowned and turned slightly. "I didn't tick you off with my questions, did I?"

"Not directly. But implications might offend some Amish."

"You ever want to go back?" He threw down the last of his drink then waited for an answer.

"I made my choice a long time ago." He hadn't given a straight answer, but he knew Jack understood what he meant. "Why are you asking about this?" Jack had mentioned the community occasionally in the past, though not like he had been lately. He chuckled. Maybe he was admiring the Amish more than he realized.

"What are you laughing about?"

"You. Why are you so curious all of a sudden?"

He stuck out his bottom lip and thought for a second. "I can't see you ever being there is all."

"That's because you've never seen me there. It's a lot different."

"I know, that's why I was asking. You must have hated it a lot to leave. I would have."

"It's a good place to live, just... different."

"Whatever you say. Can't imagine you there though."

Jack's comments were becoming even more irritating. He was used to those in the secular world making fun of the Amish, but he still didn't like to hear people talk badly about them.

They paid the tab and walked to the parking lot. Daniel was deep in thought. He tried not to think of his time in the community. Too many bad memories. The former bishop always seemed to hold a grudge against his father. Maybe it was just his perception as a teenage boy but there was something amiss. That he knew.

"Hey, you good to drive?" Jack asked, watching him intently.

"I'm fine. Long day, you know the drill."

Jack nodded "All right then. See you tomorrow?"

"I have some errands to run; I have the late shift." They said good-bye. Daniel slid his legs under the steering wheel and started the engine. He wasn't looking forward to being at the hospital today. It usually didn't bother him, but he found his thoughts returning to the community—especially to the Amish moms, whose needs were so great. He thought about the words Fannie had blurted out and contemplated the truth of them. He wanted to provide all he could of what they needed, especially this time of year. But did he have it in him? Was Fannie right?

Amish mothers had few options if complications arose. It made their cases more urgent than those of women who could go to a hospital. There were exceptions of course, but for the most part the Amish women just worked their way through the problems.

It never ceased to surprise him how the community women helped expectant mothers get through the birthing experience. It was simple and there was usually nothing out of the ordinary, especially with the Amish women encouraging one another to make it as comfortable as possible. No one did birthing better in his opinion.

His thoughts turned to Jack. They'd known each other for years, but lately things seemed to have changed. Or maybe it was just him. Either way, he felt uneasy as he wrestled with what was going on around him. Something was stirring, no doubt about it. But was it physical or mental?

What about the strange tremor he had experienced earlier? He'd been getting only a few hours of sleep over the last week. Perhaps the stress was starting to catch up with him. Maybe his irritation with Jack was a manifestation of that same stress.

Once the spring newborns were safely delivered, things would settle down and life would go back to normal. But just what that would look like he wasn't sure.

As he pulled into his garage, his phone rang. He checked the number. It was the community phone.

He imagined Fannie in the small Amish-made telephone booth. The way it was designed couldn't be more uncomfortable, and Daniel wondered if it wasn't done on purpose to keep people from talking too much. It was for emergencies only, but he hoped they'd be a little more lenient this time of year.

He quickly answered. "Dr. Kauffman, who is calling?"

"Daniel, it's Fannie." Her breath was rapid and shaky. "Thank goodness you answered."

"Do you have a delivery?"

"*Jah*. Are you home?"

"I'm about twenty minutes away." He wanted to ask who it was, what was going on, but couldn't waste the time.

"I don't know if it will be mother or child but one of them is going to exhaust themselves real quick if someone doesn't get down here and soon. I can't—"

"I'm on my way, ETA. . . ." He stopped. Threw out the medical jargon and started again. "I'll be there as quickly as possible. Meantime, remember in our business there are no such words as 'I can't.'" He paused. "You can do this, Fannie."

He wiped his brow with his hand, wishing he had an

experienced assistant already prepping so he didn't have to do it when he got there.

But Fannie was there, so maybe things would work out all right.

Chapter Five

Fannie's hands shook as she held the phone to her ear. Although she'd been assisting Daniel for a while now, she'd never been alone with a *mamm* during a delivery, been solely in charge. *I can do this,* she told herself. *I can do this.*

"I'll get there as fast as I can. Hang on." Daniel's voice was calm, soothing. Fannie felt as nervous as the expectant mother. Daniel might be stubborn, but tonight he was showing her a different side. He was kind and encouraging. Encouraging? Was this the same Daniel?

"*Ach*, I'll do my best. But hurry."

"If you're worried, the mother will worry too, so stay strong." He paused, and then added, "It's not like you to be any other way."

She blinked, not expecting his confidence in her. "*Jah*, but I need someone with experience beside me."

"Picture me beside you, supporting you step-by-step. I know you can do this."

His demeanor calmed her for a moment. "*Jah*, okay."

"Fannie, you will be fine."

She drew in a long breath and ended the call, feeling better about facing the task without him.

The temperature had dropped during her short time talking to Daniel. Spring was taking its time creeping in.

She'd been in the garden when the message arrived that Mrs. Unruh was going into labor. Not long ago the couple had moved from a smaller community to be closer to his family.

Fannie knocked once and opened the front door. "*Hallo* there."

"*Ach*, *gut*. You're assisting Doc, ya?" The father closed the door behind her and led the way.

"Actually I'm a midwife. Dr. Daniel will be here soon."

His face tightened. "So you know how to care for my wife?" He walked quickly, leading her down the hall.

"I'm learning—"

The young man stopped, looked at her, and kept walking. "Maybe we should wait for one of the doctors."

She walked past him and stopped. "I've helped bring over a dozen babies into this world. I suggest you let me help while we wait."

His brows lifted, then he turned and stepped into the last room on the left where a young woman lay, as jumpy as a rabbit.

"Thank goodness, someone is here." Her thick red hair, wet with moisture, was tucked behind her ears. "Where's the doc?"

Her husband answered from the doorway before Fannie had a moment to explain. "Doc's on his way. He'll get here in time."

Fannie had learned to be straightforward to avoid any

misunderstanding. "Dr. Daniel is on his way, but if he's delayed, you and I will bring this child into the world."

"Ahh!" The young woman cringed. The fear in her eyes told Fannie that the doctor's possible delay made her even more fearful and stressed. She writhed with pain, caught her breath with a grimace, and cried out. Fannie spun into action. She hurried for the towels stacked at the foot of the bed on a trunk next to a bowl of cold water.

"Can I help?" The young husband stood at the doorway, as white-faced and jittery as his wife. He seemed to want to keep his distance.

"It would be helpful if you'd bring us a bowl of hot water, a cup of red raspberry tea, a..."

His eyes widened with each item she requested, so she backed off. If he was too uncomfortable to come in the room, he wouldn't be any help to her.

"Better yet, why don't you keep an eye out for the doctor and get him in here as soon as possible."

When he heard the doctor was still on his way the young man's shoulders slumped a little. He nodded and took off down the hallway.

"It's better that he's gone." The mother-to-be seemed a little more relaxed until another contraction made her writhe and cry out.

"Good. With each contraction you get a little closer." Fannie was going with whatever she could remember of what she'd learned when watching Daniel. Now she almost regretted the time she'd spent cleaning dishes and calming other family members instead of paying more attention to his deliveries.

Maybe that was what worried her. She hadn't enough

practice with the actual delivery, just getting the *mamms* prepared and holding their hands. She'd seen dozens of deliveries and helped midwives but had never been on her own for the entire birthing process.

The sound of boots on the wood floors gave her hope Daniel had arrived. When she looked up though, the young father stood there with a cold cloth.

The young man nodded. "Sure you don't need anything else?"

"Be strong. It's the best thing you can do for her and yourself." She smiled to show him she wasn't worried. But she knew that if Daniel didn't show up soon, she would be.

Taking a deep breath, she checked to see the mother's dilation. The baby appeared to be turned.

Fannie wondered how the young *mamm* would receive the information.

"What's your name?" she asked.

"Leah." She sagged against her pillows.

"Well, Leah, Dr. Daniel is going to help the babe out." Where was he? Surely it had been long enough. She fought to keep her panic out of voice by breathing evenly and deeply.

The *mamm* unconsciously mimicked Fannie's breathing and smiled.

Her husband had returned and this time entered the room, though tentatively. He was holding another damp cloth and handed it to Fannie. "Does the doctor do things our way? He's at a hospital now, right?"

"Husband, I don't care who delivers this child, just so it happens soon." The mother winced and tightened.

"Another contraction?" Fannie gave Leah a calm smile.

Leah nodded as she panted her way through the pain.

"First time?" Fannie asked as she put the cloth on her forehead, making conversation. There were no signs of children in the house, but she might have miscarried.

"*Jah*, the first. I thought...getting kicked by a horse...was bad. That's nothing...compared to this." Sweat rolled down her forehead, and Fannie wiped it away.

"What else can I do to help, to make you more comfortable?" The young husband looked like he wanted to run away, and fast.

"Nothing, Jakob. I'm fine here with Fannie." She averted her eyes, maybe embarrassed or she just wanted to do this alone.

Fannie could almost see the modesty in her eyes. "You'll be close by then?" she said to the father, hoping he caught her meaning.

"*Ach*, sure. I'll be in the hallway if you need me." He kissed Leah on the cheek, then smiled and turned to go.

Fannie preferred the father to be there to encourage the *mamm* if possible, but it was not uncommon for the *mamm* to rely on the midwife.

I can do this. I can do this, she told herself. She sincerely wished Daniel was beside her but a part of her also wanted to prove to herself that she could do it alone.

"I think I'm ready." The woman leaned her head against the pillow, as if waiting for Fannie to perform the birth right at that minute.

She placed her hands on the woman's large stomach and felt the taut skin and the strain beneath it. Between that and the consistent groan, she seemed ready to deliver. No time to waste.

"Take some deep breaths and hold my hand if you need to." Fannie hoped she didn't. She'd witnessed some new *mamms* squeezing so hard the midwife cried out in pain.

Her mind started working double-time. What if a caesarian was needed?

Another groan from the mother brought Fannie back to the reality at hand. Fannie drew in a deep breath and gave Leah another smile, then began to prep her for delivery.

"I'm ready. This babe feels ready." The *mamm* tried to smile but seemed to lose her energy as quickly as it came.

"I'm going to agree with you on that." They exchanged smiles just as a commotion carried toward them from downstairs.

Please, Lord, let this be Daniel.

Seconds later the husband tapped on the door.

"Doc's been spotted in the area. Hold on, hon." The young man kissed the back of her hand and pulled away. Leah nodded and wiped a trickle of sweat off her forehead.

Another knock sounded downstairs, and the father rushed to answer the door.

When Daniel appeared a moment later, dismay filled Fannie. He looked exhausted. As tired as the new *mamm*.

"How are we?" Daniel set down his bag then rolled up his sleeves.

As soon as he said the words, she felt her confidence blossom again. "I think the baby is ready to be turned."

She used soft words so as not to alarm the parents.

Finally, hours of cries and tears and pain later, they heard a rooster crow just as the baby made her way into the world.

"A nice touch," Daniel murmured, almost to himself. "It seems fitting that an Amish baby makes its appearance at daybreak. A fresh start for everyone."

Daniel washed his hands in a basin beside the bed and threw the towel over his left shoulder. Then he handed the little one to Fannie to wrap up in a pink blanket. As the mother and father shifted into a comfortable position, a strange feeling came over Fannie that she couldn't describe.

"*Ach*, Dr. Daniel. Thank goodness. I thought sure you weren't gonna get here in time." The young father looked with admiration at the doc.

"We'd have hated to do this without you. First one, ya know." The chatty couple turned their attention to the little one Fannie brought to them. They both grinned from ear to ear.

"Look how small her fingers are." The beaming mother wouldn't let her go and didn't stop touching the tiny one.

Fannie cleaned up while letting them coo over their new family member.

"Grab that cloth and wrap it up." Daniel spoke to Fannie with his regular bluntness. But this time it seemed like something else. Although Daniel was a serious man, she'd occasionally seen a softness about him like what she had witnessed just a few moments before.

"We're done here for today. I'll be back tomorrow, but if anything changes let me know."

"Thank you, Doctor." The father barely lifted his eyes from his daughter. Any doubts about Daniel seemed to have disappeared once seeing him in action.

"You're very welcome." Daniel picked up his bag and nodded. "You'll be billed accordingly."

Fannie was still new to working with Daniel but didn't know if she'd ever get used to his demeanor toward his patients. "I'll stay awhile to see that everyone is comfortable."

He glanced over his shoulder at the young parents before stepping through the door. They looked exhausted but were still smiling. His gaze then met Fannie's before he turned and left the room.

Chapter Six

Watching Fannie handle the delivery brought out a side of Daniel he didn't realize he had. Performing surgery always put him on guard. But deliveries were quite different.

It's something he ever expected when choosing a specialty in medical school. Of course he should have known better. Delivering Amish babies reminded him how different the process was in their community versus the clinical atmosphere in hospitals. He was also beginning to realize his expertise in the area was directly related to his background. He knew the Amish ways.

He parked his car in his personalized parking place at the hospital and as he got out, spotted a smudge on the hood. As he stopped to wipe it off, he was struck by how his focus changed outside the community, and not always for the good. He drew his hand back, aware of the materialism that surrounded him. That he'd bought into.

"You get a ding?" Jack came up behind him.

Daniel turned. "Nah, just a little dirt."

Jack frowned and stepped closer to inspect. "I keep

telling you that you should stay away from the black. Silver is the way to go."

Daniel smiled good-naturedly at his friend. "You have a lot of surgeries today?"

Daniel knew that Jack's schedule had been so full lately he was in danger of burning out or making a mistake.

Jack shrugged and let out a short laugh. "Yeah, I have two houses to pay for and a cabin in the Rocky Mountains."

"Sounds like the lifestyle of the rich and famous."

"What can I say? Women love exotic places. I'm looking to get into an apartment in California. Women in swimsuits." He waggled his eyebrows, and Daniel lost a little more respect for him. It was time to change the conversation.

"See you in there." He nodded toward the large hospital and thought about how different it was than from treating patients in their homes.

"You in a hurry?" Jack picked up his stride and turned one way as Daniel went the other.

"Yeah, see you." His thoughts stopped, and he took in the spring air as he approached the building.

"Stay positive." He mumbled to himself as he walked in the door and felt the brisk air the building expelled.

The lavish entryway was impressive with its modern art and large plants on each side of the entry. The rich coffee scent from the Starbucks down the hall wafted through to the cafeteria that served food almost as good as some four-star restaurants.

"Dr. Kauffman, long time, no see." Jessica, a cute

young nurse, put a hand on her hip, shamelessly showing off her slim figure.

"There are a lot of babies due this spring." He smiled, and she smiled wider.

"I just can't imagine working with those women, delivering with none of them using any anesthesia." She went on, and he was gone, thinking of Fannie and how he'd never heard her complain about any of the issues that came up outside the community.

"Doctor." She tilted her head, frowning. "You're not listening."

"Oh, sorry."

He made his way to surgery, stopping along the way to check the board to see what activity had been done, what was next, and who was taking each task. He felt like he was part of a flock of sheep following whoever was in charge that day.

When he got to his office, he stopped. Fannie stood, her back to him, looking over his diplomas, among other plaques and certificates of accomplishments.

For a second he felt self-conscious, knowing how the Amish felt about showing others their achievements.

"I didn't expect you here."

When she turned to him, she seemed only slightly out of place. Her confidence alone shone through her green eyes and was enough to dispel any discomfort she might have.

"It's not like I visit frequently outside the community, especially here." She returned his stare, and he realized it was his turn to keep the conversation going.

"Is there something wrong?" He frowned, wondering why he didn't ask that right off.

"I'm not sure." She leaned her head to one side and kept her eyes on his. "I know you're busy, but I felt we should talk a moment about your manner."

"My manner?" He frowned, not liking her implication. He had an excellent bedside manner. Everyone said so.

"*Jah.*" She pursed her lips and paused. "You're a bit abrupt. Folks are offended that you mention billing before the baby has started to nurse."

She waited for his response.

Her expression said this was hard for her, coming to him with criticism, especially since what money she earned came from those payments. "Well then, I appreciate your candor. I will endeavor to use more of my compassionate training when I'm called to a birth." She seemed to want to say more but was hesitating. "Is there something else on your mind?"

"I know you can't promise regular visits because of your responsibilities here, but you're leaving me with a lot of duties—prenatal checks and the simpler births." She lifted a brow and kept her frown.

"If you get in a bind, let me know." He felt he was being fair but by the look on her face she wasn't convinced.

"And you're comfortable with that?"

As much of a pain as she was, still he admired her. She put the patient first, which was the way it should be. "Okay then, I'll see what I can squeeze into my schedule. Fair enough?"

A small smile was all he got but that was enough. That meant a lot coming from her.

"I feel better already, *danke.*" She moved forward and held out her hand.

"A handshake?" He grinned, then realized that might be patronizing. Too late.

Fannie took a step back and gathered her shawl. "Sorry." She disappeared out his office door.

She had been gone just a moment when his doorway was filled with the charge nurse.

"You've been gone a lot lately." Cindy put her hands on her hips, swinging her blonde ponytail over her shoulder.

It was obvious she thought she was cute as a button. They'd worked together a long time and had always gotten along. Once in a while Daniel thought he caught her looking at him with an odd, almost hungry expression, but he'd probably imagined it. He didn't date. Everyone knew that. Not since Emily.

"There are a number of babies due this spring." He grinned and she did too.

"I see. How's it going?"

"Good. You know I like doing this." He smiled genially.

"I get jealous sometimes." She tilted her head to one side.

"Why? Everyone around here thinks I'm nuts for spending more time for less money."

"Some people only think of one thing." She paused. "You don't."

He grunted. "You're biased."

"I'm a sucker for a rebel." She handed him a file. "Are you ever going to use the computer?"

"Only when I have to. But I don't hate the new technology as much as I used to."

She laughed. "That's because half the time you do it all the old-fashioned way."

"You're just jealous."

"I said I was. But I'm also impressed. Now what am I going to do with the extra time I used to use on you?"

"I don't remember us having any time." He grinned.

"That's my point." Her eyes caught his and held. She tilted her head. "Do you want to have dinner together?"

He gulped. He didn't date. She knew that. Everyone in the hospital knew it. Work was his life. Relationships weren't.

"If it takes you that long to decide, I presume it's a no." She waited another moment then turned away.

"Yes." Where did that come from? He didn't plan on saying it. The word just burst forth like flood water bursting a dam.

She shrugged.

He scrambled for words, any words. "When and where?"

She would probably know where to go better than he would. He was terrible at this. Married too long ago and not having dated in years made him feel awkward around attractive women. Unless being with Fannie counted.

"It's up to you."

"Okay, how about Sergio's? Do you like Italian?" He hoped it was a yes because it had been too painful to get this far.

"I like Italian. Sergio's it is. Friday?" She smiled, but it didn't reach her eyes. A floor nurse stepped in. She nodded and handed a chart to Daniel, then kept walking.

"Thanks." He lifted one side of his cheek then returned his attention toward Cindy. An image of his deceased wife flashed before him. It always did when he had an opportunity to spend time with another woman.

"See you Friday then." He lifted his hand and turned away, waiting for the picture of Emily to flash again. Then to his surprise, Fannie's image popped into his mind instead.

Chapter Seven

Young James Miller was grinning to beat the band as he waved good-bye to Fannie. Goodness, one would have thought she'd invited him for breakfast. Instead, as usual, he'd invited himself over under the pretense of dropping by some sausage. He always timed it perfectly, just after the milking was done and *Mamm* and *Mammi* were setting the table.

She waved back and was about to close the door when she saw Daniel's pickup truck making its way to the *haus*, puffs of dust trailing. The little burst of joy from somewhere in her heart surprised her.

She untied her apron, ran back to the kitchen, and tossed it toward its hook. *Mamm* and *Mammi* looked at her quizzically.

"Daniel," she said as she hurried past them but not before she saw the two women exchange glances.

She had just stepped outside when Daniel got out of the pickup.

For a moment he just stood there in the early morning sunlight, and the look of him nearly took her breath away. How could this be? This was Daniel. He irritated her to no end. Why was her heart doing crazy flip-flops? She felt her cheeks warm, and she drew in a deep, calming breath.

"Do we have another delivery?"

"Yes, Sarah Zook. But she's in good hands. Her family is with her, and the contractions are still far apart." He took a few steps closer to Fannie. "We need to talk." He inclined his head toward the porch swing with a quizzical look.

"This sounds serious."

"Yes, please, let's sit."

He followed her back up the steps to the swing, and held it still while she settled into it. They would have sat very close if he'd joined her. Too close. But she didn't need to worry. Daniel pulled the rocker closer to the swing and sat.

He leaned forward earnestly and lifted his brows, his gaze capturing hers. "You're good at what you do. You're especially good with the mothers."

Her eyebrows shot up. Could he really be complimenting her?

He went on. "I would like to give you more responsibility. I'd like you to keep working with deliveries, but I'd also like you to take on the post-birth visits, at least through spring if that works for you."

"We would still be working together?"

"Yes."

"I will need to think about it."

He let out a long sigh and sat back in the rocker, his eyes still searching hers.

"You caught me unaware. It's one thing to help you with deliveries, but to make regular visits to *mamms* after the babes are born is different. I still have chores to do, and I work at the bakery some mornings."

He drummed his fingers on the arm of the rocking-chair. "I've given a lot of my time to be available for the community. I thought you felt the same." He frowned and looked away from her before continuing. "You're a good nurse. Doc was the one who first told me about your skills." He grinned, suddenly looking boyish. "And when Doc speaks, I have to listen."

He looked out at the fields, lit by the morning sun, and when he spoke, it seemed he was almost talking to himself. "I'm asking you as a favor, Fannie. I need some breathing room. There's just too much for me to do just now." He swiped his hand through his hair and looked back at her. His fatigue was evident in his eyes. She noticed a slight tremor in his hand just before he rested it on the arm of the rocker.

"More babies than usual," she mused. "And you need more time at the hospital and here." Her heart when out to him, no matter how much he irritated her. "Simple as that." How could she say no? She sat back in the swing, letting it rock her gently.

He half grinned and cocked one eyebrow. She couldn't help but laugh at the gesture. It looked like something he might have done as a boy.

But it still nagged her that he might not truly believe in her abilities but was asking for her help simply because she was his only option.

"Well?" he said.

"Maybe I need time to think it over." She was half joking, maybe just wanting to know how badly he wanted her to help.

He sighed again and rolled his eyes. "While you're thinking it through, answer me this. Are you betrothed?"

"What?" She never thought she would be considered to be betrothed and was even more surprised that Daniel had asked the question. "Why do you ask?"

Daniel inclined his head toward the road then looked at her. "I just passed James Miller leaving your house, looking like he was walking on air. It made me wonder...makes me wonder...if that's one of the reasons you don't want to give up any more of your time."

Fannie briefly wondered if there might be a hint of jealousy in him. But that didn't seem like Daniel.

"James has been that way for as long as I've known him."

"So your answer is...?"

She stood, brushed off her skirt, nodded toward his truck. "We're wasting daylight, and Sarah Zook's time is likely upon us."

She took off down the porch steps, grinning as he trotted to catch up. "So is that a yes?" he called after her.

Chapter Eight

Another day and Fannie still hadn't given him a definite answer, which irritated him to no end. The Amish had their own sense of time, usually agonizingly slow, but as a doctor, he couldn't afford to slow down. And to top it off, this morning she was later than usual, still milking the cows when he arrived to pick her up.

He steered the pickup onto the road, taking the corner faster than usual.

"You're angry." She kept her eyes straight ahead. Her expression seemed to say she didn't care if he was angry or not. She finally turned to him, fixing her gorgeous green eyes on his face, a half smile playing at the corner of her lips.

He almost swerved off the road.

He cleared his throat. "This can't happen again..." He let the last words trail out. Those green eyes had almost done him in.

"What can't happen again?"

"You need to be on time, ready at the time I say. I don't have the time to wait for you." He kept his gaze on the road so her eyes wouldn't make him lose his train of thought again.

She sounded indignant when she spoke. "For your information, I do have other things to occupy my time. I could be making money selling food in the stands to the tourists."

He pursed his lips, not daring to look at her again. "Then maybe that's what you should do." He usually did very well ignoring people who irritated him, but it was different with her. That red hair and those green eyes conspired to make him forget himself.

"What do you think the Amish *mamms* do here when there's no doctor around?" She sounded amused rather than upset. Why wasn't she taking him seriously?

"What they've always done, birth babies with help from other women."

"Indeed," she said.

He tried to be patient. "Times have changed. So much more can be done about the pain, much more than relying on the herbs Doc Rueben uses." He was making too much of this, but she knew how to keep him going with her rebuttals.

"You sure have come a long way from your time among the Amish." She rolled down the window and let the air hit her face.

"I've had to. It's like I've been jumping back and forth from the present to the past and back again." He doubted she could understand. As they passed farmlands and pastures, he drew in a deep, calming breath. Looking out across the fields, this place seemed more like home to him than did the city.

They remained quiet until they drove up to the white

house with black trim next to a large vegetable garden. He rested his arms on the steering wheel and took it all in. It wasn't as if he'd never seen a garden before, but for whatever reason this one caught his eye. It reminded him of home, and feelings long buried seemed to creep up from someplace deep inside.

Since his little lecture about time, Fannie now seemed to have gained a new perspective. He was still taking in the garden when she almost leaped out of the vehicle. When he didn't follow her lead, she shut the door and walked to the house.

She looked back at him when she got to the front door. "Are you coming?"

He grinned as he stepped out and shut the door. "Anybody home?"

Fannie cupped her hands and looked through the door. "I see someone." She waved him over. The door opened, and a young man stood before her.

"Thank *Gott*, you're here. Come in, please." He waved a hand and stopped when he saw Daniel.

"*Hallo* there." By the look on his face he wasn't sure why Daniel was there, though it should have been obvious. "Haven't seen you in a while."

"Forgive me, I'm not sure I remember..." Daniel was suddenly sorry he couldn't place all the Amish he met during his visits, but it was inevitable. He'd been gone too long.

"You must remember my uncle, though. Jeremiah." He gestured for them to enter the house.

"Oh, yes. I should have known; I see the resemblance." Jeremiah was a bit older than Daniel, but they spent a lot of time together. He hoped he didn't tell his nephew everything about their teen years. They'd been a bit rambunctious back then. "Your uncle and I spent a lot of time together."

Sam led the way down a hall to the mother-to-be lying on her bed and stayed in the hallway.

Just before Fannie stepped into the room, she glanced at Daniel, tipping her cheek to one side with a small smile. He smiled at the gesture, imagining how she may have looked as a girl.

Bess, the young mother-to-be, was petite, which in proportion made her stomach seem even larger. She was obviously uncomfortable. "I'm Dr. . . ." He paused for a moment, used to the formality of using his last name with his patients at the hospital. "Dr. Daniel."

Fannie's nod said she understood. "He works at the hospital and helps us now that Doc Rueben has his hands full."

"Let's see how you're doing." Daniel took out his stethoscope and listened to her heart.

Fannie sat down near the bed and reached for the young woman's hand. "I've missed you at church service. Let me know if you'd like for me to read some Bible passages to you. I've gotten pretty good at it with all of these babies on their way and the *mamms* without much to do but listen." She smiled in such a comforting way the woman's heart rate slowed slightly.

"I would like that," Bess said.

"You're fine," Daniel said. "Your heart is working hard, but it sounds healthy. Just take it as easy as you can."

"I don't have much choice these days." She grimaced as she tried to move her body to a sitting position and then leaned back against the headboard. "I hope it's a girl." That made her smile and her husband grunt.

Daniel snapped the latch on his satchel. "You're doing well. I know you're uncomfortable, but the baby is not quite ready."

Fannie gave an awkward hug to Bess and led the way to the door.

Daniel stopped and turned to Sam, who stood just outside the room. "How is your dad these days?"

He smiled. "He's good. Excited about the new babe."

Daniel smiled, thinking of Jeremiah's older brother as a grandfather.

Sam looked down at his boots then back up at Daniel. "I was sorry to hear about your *mamm* and *daed*." His voice was low. "I try to keep an eye out in case your *mamm* needs anything. We all do."

Daniel was grateful the community had been so good to his mom. "Thanks, Sam. I really appreciate it."

The Amish kept things to themselves as much as they could, and in this way Daniel had not changed. He hoped his silence meant that was the end of it.

Fannie watched the exchange and decided to help Daniel a little. "Take care, Sam, and let us know if anything changes." Fannie kept them moving down the hallway and then outside toward the truck.

But Sam followed and caught up with Daniel. "I just wanted to thank you for what you're doing. I know the bishop wasn't easy on you back when you left, and now…"

Daniel stopped and turned to him. "I appreciate that, Sam. But I'm not here for the bishop. I'm here for

Bess and the other mothers who need help with their deliveries."

"*Jah.*" Sam nodded. "Well, *danke* just the same."

Sam started back to the house.

Fannie walked by and gave him a quizzical look before getting in his vehicle.

He hoped she'd tread lightly and not ask too many questions about what she'd heard. It seemed she could read his thoughts because as he pulled the pickup away from the house, she just stared straight ahead.

Chapter Nine

Jannie's heart was heavy when leaving the couple's home. She hadn't really considered how hard it may be for Daniel to come back and face the community again. The bishop was difficult enough, but everyone also knew his *mamm* and *daed* lived apart, which was rarely done.

The silence thickened around them; even the sunlight seemed dim.

When she couldn't take the quiet any longer, she glanced over at him. "What happened between you and your *daed* the other day?" She guessed he was the one Daniel had been arguing with at the run-down house on the hill. She didn't know what it was like to be at odds with her family. A couple spats here or there with her sisters but nothing like the raised voices she'd overheard at that house. None of their words were really clear, but their tones said it all.

Daniel's jaw tightened and his eyes didn't leave the road. He rubbed his head until his brown hair stood on end, then he reached over and began to massage his elbow. He glanced at her, then at his hand, then back to the road.

When he didn't answer, she decided to change the subject.

"One more and we're done for the day."

He kept his gaze ahead. "I'm done for the day now, Fannie."

His lack of inflection told her not to push, but they couldn't keep the babies from coming or stop the checkups.

She hesitated and then said, "There are three more on the list for tomorrow."

"We'll worry about that later." His usual bright blue eyes were a glassy haze, but she couldn't tell if he was mad or sad, and she knew he probably didn't want to talk about anything that just happened.

"But it's baby season. We're very busy."

He kept driving, and at first it seemed as if he hadn't heard her.

"I'm aware of that, but I have something pressing to take care of." He worked his jaw as he tore down the dirt road, to the point that it made her uneasy.

"Daniel, will you please slow down?" She pushed her feet against the floorboard as he got off the dirt road and onto the two-lane highway, the truck fish-tailing on the pavement. That's when she had to do something.

"Stop!" she shouted.

He slammed on the brakes, and they skidded to a standstill.

The basket of home-cooked sweets, made for the last family on the day's roster, fell from her lap to the floor.

"What is wrong with you, Daniel?" She started

picking up the food, disgusted at the loss of the hard-earned goodies a weary *mamm* would appreciate.

He wiped his palm over a face that needed a good shave. "Sorry, I shouldn't be driving."

"I'd say. What came over you?" She placed the last of the muffins in her basket, willing her disgust to dissipate.

"Old ghosts. I have many here." He didn't seem to want to elaborate. He pressed the accelerator again, but more gently. They stayed within the speed limit as he drove them toward the ramshackle house on the hill again.

She was too curious to leave the matter alone. "Ghosts of what? Your *daed*? Your wife?" Fannie watched him intently.

He finally looked over at her with pain in his eyes. She wasn't sure if what she saw there was defeat, disappointment, or something she could only imagine. She wanted to console him, but she didn't know how or what for, or if he would accept her concern.

"I need to make a stop." He wouldn't meet her eyes, nor did she want him to. She wouldn't know what to say.

"Whatever you need."

He put his elbow against the window and looked at the countryside rolling by, neat rows of crops dotted by houses and barns. "Just give me a minute."

He rubbed his elbow with such force he seemed to be wrestling with something bigger than his *daed*, his *daed*'s friend, and his relationship with his *daed*. But there was no clue as to what it was or why she didn't know something more about them.

"It must be hard coming back to a place you don't

want to be." The words came from nowhere, meant to be a thought in her mind not spoken.

When he didn't respond she laid a hand on his arm. "Can I pray for you, with whatever you're struggling with?"

"No." His voice was higher and his patience short.

Fannie sat back in the seat and told herself to let it go, reminded herself that this wasn't personal, but found it not so easy.

She could hear his breath rise and fall as he turned toward her. "On second thought, it's best you not be there. I'll take you home." He seemed irritated yet determined, which confused her even more, so she let it alone.

"I'll do this another day." He pulled to the side of the road and glanced behind so he could turn around.

She laid a hand on his. "Whatever it is that troubles you should be taken care of. If not today, then when?"

He seemed more than confused as to what he should do, but to her it was obvious. He sighed then continued up the rutted road. After turning off the truck, he glanced at the beaten down wooden home then back to her. "I'll be right back. Don't get out of the pickup." His eyes froze into hers and didn't blink until she nodded.

He opened the door and stepped out, then took a breath. "Whatever you hear, don't come in."

She frowned, concerned even more.

He whipped his head toward her with a frown. "I mean it. Stay put." His glare was almost scary, but she doubted he meant to be. Even if he did, she wouldn't show him her fear, for him or his *daed*.

"I will stay outside as long as I don't think you're in

danger." She didn't look at him. She knew his expression without facing him.

"Don't be so dramatic. I'll be in and out." With that he slammed the door behind him. When he got to the porch, he pointed for her to stay where she was.

After a minute had gone by, she heard voices. The sound grew louder until she could tell they were shouting. She reached for the pickup door.

She was just about to get out of the truck when she heard Daniel's boots hitting the wood floor and then out on the porch. When he saw her sitting in the truck with the door open on her side he pursed his lips and took the steps two at a time.

He opened the door and shut it then reached over to shut hers. "What was the one thing I asked you not to do?"

Fannie was too confused to reply right away, which was uncommon for her. When she gathered herself together she let out a long breath and turned to him.

There were so many more emotions going around them she decided not to speak. When she looked over at him she noticed his chest rise and fall and his eyes close.

She instinctively touched his hand and to her surprise he didn't reject her gesture. "It sounded rough in there." Before he responded, she changed the subject, thinking he probably wanted to keep whatever this was to himself. "I should be getting home."

He pulled his hand away and sat up straight, and without looking back, turned down the gravel driveway.

They drove along in a painful silence. Fannie tried to hold her tongue, but after a few minutes she couldn't help but try to reach out to him again. "I don't know what just happened, and I don't mean to intrude, but—"

He held up a hand. "There's nothing you can do, and nothing I'll try to do again. He clearly doesn't want me coming around."

"But he's your *daed*…"

"That doesn't mean he acts like it." He looked away. After a moment or so he leaned back and seemed to relax a little.

"Do you ever see him?" she asked.

He kept his eyes forward. "Before the last time we were here, not since I left the community."

"He didn't want you to be a doctor?" Those who left for such things as more education were frowned upon and asked to leave the community.

"No, he didn't want me to go to medical school, even though he knew that's what I wanted, needed, to do."

"How do you know that about him?" In the few years she'd been in the community, she'd heard that Abe Kauffman was a difficult man, but she always liked to give people the benefit of the doubt.

He turned to her. "I know you're trying to help, but it's harder than you think to get over the past, especially when it directly relates to the present."

"I can't stand to see someone unhappy."

"You're trying too hard."

"What do you mean?"

"To get my mind off of what just happened." He paused and glanced at her. "You don't have to take care of me. I knew this would happen sooner or later. I just thought it might be later rather than sooner."

She nodded. "Maybe someday you'll explain things to me." The minute she said it his demeanor chilled.

"I shouldn't have brought you. It won't happen again."

She didn't know what to do. So she took his hand and said a silent prayer.

Chapter Ten

The wind blowing and the dust whirling made for a longer walk than she expected.

"I meant to tell you that James might come by." *Mamm* didn't look at Fannie as she bustled across the kitchen, likely knowing she'd have to answer more questions than she wanted to. Her *mamm* seemed to determined to have her betrothed and married sooner than later.

"*Jah*, why is he here again?" Fannie glanced around for another task to keep busy but that wouldn't keep her *mamm* from giving her opinion on Fannie's future.

"You asked the same thing when John Graber came to visit too. You can't say no to every man who comes your way. I'm just thinking of what's best for you."

Fannie cut potatoes into chunks for mashed potatoes, hoping to distract her *mamm*, but Verna wouldn't let it go that easy. Fannie was so tired of her continuous questions she could bust.

"I'm just trying to help." Her *mamm*'s slow pace skinning potatoes told Fannie she wasn't as interested in the potatoes as in her love life. "I'm partial to James."

Fannie had heard that many times. She could hear it

coming before *Mamm* even spoke it. "*Mamm*, he's four years younger than me." A futile attempt but worth a try.

"Some people need someone older than them to learn from." She kept her eyes on the potato she was skinning so as to avoid Fannie's gaze. *Mamm* knew better than to look her in the eyes while countermanding most everything Fannie said. "I'm just trying to help." The tension in her voice told Fannie to let go of the frustration.

Fannie paused, wishing she were at their first home in Pennsylvania, where some of her relatives were.

They'd stayed here only because her sister Lucy had married a horrible man who later died in a fire. The kicker was Lucy and Manny, her new husband, moved to start over in a different community nearby.

That left her and her *mamm* here with the "girls": *Mammi* Frieda, Great-Aunt Rose, and their friend Nellie. Rose and Nellie lived in town above Nellie's quilting shop. She was so successful and busy that Fannie didn't have much time with her. And since the ache from Fannie's father's death was still fresh, *Mamm* wouldn't be leaving any time soon.

"Have you heard anything from Lucy these days?" *Mamm* asked, as if reading her mind.

Fannie frowned. "Not much. She's busy with the twins and doesn't want help from anyone. She and Manny seem to like to be alone." She suddenly felt lonely herself, with everyone gone but *Mamm*, Frieda, and her.

She stopped cutting the potatoes for a moment and gazed through the kitchen window. The low hills were covered with gold and purple wildflowers, the fields were now velvet green from earlier rains. Summer was right around the corner.

A beautiful sight but she wondered if this was where she should be. She had more family back in Tennessee, more than there would ever be here. Was this the reason she had no interest in her suitors and settling down in this community? Or was it something else that her heart was tangling with?

She'd always said she would marry if she found the right man times two. Her expectations were high, maybe too high. At least that was what everyone told her. But shouldn't she have high expectations for her husband?

"Where are you today?"

She turned from the window to see *Mamm* staring at her hard, the bowl of partially cut potatoes in her hand.

"All over the place. Sorry, I've been doing a lot of thinking." Having someone notice her change in demeanor meant she was thinking too much. Whatever would be would be, as Frieda would say.

"About what?" Frieda took the last step down the stairway, holding the wall. This was the first time Fannie noticed that her balance seemed off. Maybe she just felt unsteady because of the slippery, finely cleaned floors.

"Fannie's beau." *Mamm* went over to Frieda and held out her hand.

She no sooner put out her hand than Frieda slapped it away. "*Ach*, what's that for?"

Verna turned back toward the kitchen with furrowed brows. If it had been anyone else, Verna would have given them a tongue lashing.

Fannie watched out of the corner of her eye to see if *Mammi* could make her way around the corner. Just as she turned, Frieda lost her balance and fell to the ground, hard.

"Ahhh!" Frieda reached down and clutched her hip, then rocked side to side. Fannie was by her *Mammi*'s side in a flash.

"Try to lie still." Fannie placed her hand lightly on the leg Frieda grasped and slowly moved it up to see where the hip was the most painful.

Fannie knew it was something serious for Frieda to be making such a fuss. It wasn't like her to complain.

Frieda clenched her jaw when Fannie touched the tender spot.

"You need a doctor."

Frieda waved her hands. "*Nee*, just give me some ice, and I'll be fine."

Fannie watched her pinch her lips together and knew she did very well need a doctor. But who? Did she ask for the community doc or Daniel?

Whoever would do the best work. After seeing Daniel in action, she was beginning to sway his way. But what would everyone in the community say?

Birthing babies was one thing, but expanding his practice in the community beyond that might create a problem.

"I'll let Doc Rueben know we need him." Verna started for the door giving Fannie little time to decide what to do.

"What about Daniel?" Fannie asked.

Frieda turned back, staring at her. Her grandmother's jaw dropped. She looked far from happy.

"I think he'd be better for this. But the first thing we need to do is to get you up off the floor and comfortable." It would be difficult to carry her up the stairs. "The couch will have to do."

Frieda scowled. "I let you do a lot of things but letting you two carry me like a sack of corn isn't one of them."

Mamm let out a sigh and Fannie put her hands on her hips. "It's not that far," she said to herself more than to Frieda.

Fannie didn't realize how heavy her grandmother was until she and her *mamm* carried her into the living room. She was still considering which doctor to get as she trotted upstairs for a quilt and a pillow. When she returned, her grandmother's face was paler than before, and her forehead was beaded with perspiration.

"That settles it. I'm going for Daniel."

Verna snapped her head up and frowned. "Birthing babies is one thing but healing a hip is another."

"Daniel does more than deliver babies." The instant response may have been too much, but *Mamm*'s perspective wasn't accurate. Fannie was getting an idea of how he might feel about his regard in the community.

Frieda chimed in. "Well, right at this moment I don't care one way or another. Just get me a doc. I don't care who it is."

"I'll keep her comfortable," *Mamm* said. "Get whoever is closer."

Fannie gave Frieda one last look and headed toward Doc's, hoping she would see Daniel along the way. He was going to be in the community sometime today, she just wasn't sure when.

She had walked only a short distance when she spotted his pickup in front of the Holster's place. It was hard to miss among all the buggies on the gravel roads.

As she approached the *haus*, she noticed the front

window was open wide. She could see Daniel inside and a young woman standing beside him. From the way she was dressed, Fannie guessed she was an *Englischer.* She hesitated. Daniel hadn't asked for her assistance today; he obviously had someone to take her place.

That was bad enough. But what if this woman was more than an assistant? She hadn't thought to ask Daniel if he was seeing someone. Not that he would have told her.

She was surprised at how much the thought bothered her. She took a deep breath and walked closer to the *haus.*

Her grandmother needed a doctor. That's all she needed to think about right now.

Chapter Eleven

Sarah Holster opened the front door. "Fannie, what are you doing out there? Is there a birthing?"

"*Nee.*" The noise seeped out before she could catch it and now she was tongue-tied. There was no escape.

"Sorry to bother. I was looking for some help with *Mammi.*"

"Well, you're in the right place. Daniel is here. I'll fetch him for you." She was gone before Fannie could say another word.

Daniel came out too quickly for her to put her words together. He frowned and made his way to her quickly. "Are you all right?"

The touch of his hand was the final thing that brought her to tears. She hated the vulnerability, but there was no way to stop even a bit of emotion. "It's *Mammi.* She's fallen and is in a bad way." She hoped he wasn't looking at her, but she needed to lift her head. "Can you come and see her?"

"Straight away. Hop in. I'll be right there." He turned back to the woman she'd seen through the window.

"Cindy, we've got to go. Get in the truck." He hurried to the Holsters, who stood waiting on their porch.

Fannie climbed into the passenger's side of the pickup, then wondered if she should have let Cindy in first. She smiled at the other woman. "I'm Fannie."

The woman smiled and put out her hand, uncommon for Amish women to do but not for English women. "And I'm Cindy." They awkwardly shook, and she clambered into the middle seat in the truck. "I work with Daniel at the hospital."

Fannie turned forward again and adjusted her *kapp*. "I'm sorry for the trouble."

"Well, we couldn't stay there." Cindy's voice was not as empathetic as Fannie expected. Did she have more important things to do?

Fannie almost bit her tongue to keep from saying something she shouldn't. "*Jah*, I suppose you're very busy at the hospital."

Cindy scoffed. "You'd think Daniel was chief of obstetrics." She turned to look at Fannie. "Did I hear that someone got hurt?"

"*Jah*, my grandmother. I think it is her hip."

"How old is she?"

Fannie looked over at her. She was looking straight out the window as if bored with the conversation.

"Older than she looks."

It was the Amish way. She'd only been in a hospital once before she visited Daniel's office and that was to help take an old neighbor of theirs who fell and broke a leg.

She turned to face Fannie. "Why you Amish don't get

medical help, I'll never understand." She caught Fannie with her blue eyes, waiting for an answer.

"The old remedies might be dismissed by the modern medicines, but they are used first." Why was she explaining the Amish way to this woman? It didn't matter what she thought.

A crunch of footsteps in the gravel carried toward them as Daniel approached the pickup and then opened the door. "Is everyone all right in here?" His gaze lingered on Fannie's face before he glanced over at Cindy and then back to Fannie.

He climbed into the cab and closed the door. "Tell me what happened," he said as he started the engine.

Fannie gave him the details of the fall and Frieda's pain afterward.

"We'll likely need to take her to the hospital," he said when she'd finished.

"I'm glad you're here." Fannie meant that in more ways than one. "I just hope you can talk *Mammi* into going to the hospital."

They hurried into the house and in just a few moments Daniel pronounced his verdict: Frieda needed X-rays. He feared her hip was broken but hoped it was just a sprain.

She was in pain, and she was ready to do just about anything necessary to receive good care, except going to the hospital. It took Fannie and Daniel several minutes to finally convince her it was the best way to get relief.

"The problem is," he said. "I'm in the truck today. I can make Frieda a bed in the back, or she can ride in front..." He let the obvious hang.

Fannie was quick to pick up on it. "I can ride in back."

Cindy shrugged.

Daniel nodded at Fannie. "Help me make a bed in the front seat. Cindy, please stay here and keep an eye on the patient."

Fannie grabbed some quilts and followed Daniel to the truck. "Thank you for taking her."

He unfolded a quilt on the seat and flashed her a smile. "It's selfish of me. I'll know she's in good hands at the hospital, and I can check in on her now and then."

He tenderly picked up Frieda and settled her on the quilts. Fannie climbed in the back, and Cindy rather reluctantly followed.

Daniel climbed into the truck and started the engine. *Mamm* waved from the porch. From the corner of her eye, Fannie saw Cindy looking at her. It wasn't like most would do, glance then look away. She just held the stare.

Fannie didn't budge, just waited for her to make the first move without looking obvious. But they had to be thinking the same thing.

The truck hit a bump in the road. "Ahh!" Cindy's voice rose, and she clutched the truck bed's side.

Fannie reached for the rear window that was half open. Riding in buggies made a vehicle seem smooth, even with a rough bout here and there.

Frieda cried out in pain.

Fannie glanced over at Cindy bouncing along and knew there was a good chance this was more than they could handle. "I think we should pull over," she called to Daniel. A part of her thought it was another chance for Daniel to give Cindy more attention, but Fannie had no reason to act like a jealous girlfriend.

The truck pulled to the side of the road.

"Let me try something first." Daniel opened his door

and stepped out to hand an extra quilt to Cindy. "Try sitting on this."

She grinned with delight and a lighthearted banter passed between the two, suddenly making Fannie feel like an intruder.

Fannie turned away, determined not to focus on the juvenile emotions that only made matters worse. She needed to focus on reality.

Footsteps sounded at the side of the truck.

Fannie craned to see who it was. James.

She'd never been so glad to see him, which surprised her.

If Daniel was courting Cindy, then Fannie had every right to be civil to James. If it made her look less pitiful, then all the better.

Chapter Twelve

When Daniel saw James he couldn't help but shake his head. James's timing was impeccable, but no matter, Daniel had a job to do. He opened Frieda's door and bent down to adjust the quilts.

The crunch of James's boots came his way and stopped in front of him. "Need any help?"

The sound of the man's voice irritated him. It was more than that, but he'd stop there. "No, but thanks." He wondered what James thought, but figured he'd only asked to be polite.

"Frieda in bad shape?" The man stooped into the truck like he was ready to fix whatever ailed her.

"I'm the one you should be asking," Frieda said. "And the answer is yes, I am in bad shape."

Daniel tucked the quilts around Frieda to make a softer bed for her hip, then stood, finding it necessary to elbow James out of the way as he did so.

"Are you all right, Daniel?" Frieda's gaze flicked from his face to his left hand.

He'd been too busy to notice his hand shaking. He

quickly covered it and forced a smile. "*Jah.* My arm is just tired."

She didn't seem convinced, but she leaned against the seat and closed her eyes.

He made his way back to the driver's side. "Okay, let me take it from here." He bumped James as he walked by. The man's nostrils flared. Daniel didn't know if it was out of anger at him or concern for Frieda. "Right now she's in shock, but she'll be better soon."

Daniel tried to determine why this man irritated him so. He'd worked with all kinds of people through the years—rich, poor, kind, and surly. He was able to tolerate most, if not all. His distinct dislike for James surprised him.

"Where are you taking her?" James asked Fannie as he leaned his elbow on the side of the truck bed.

"The hospital," Fannie said.

James swung himself into the bed of the truck. Cindy inhaled sharply. Fannie just stared at him. James glared at Daniel, almost daring him to toss him out.

Fannie gave Daniel an almost imperceptible nod. So he climbed back into the cab and headed down the road again.

Fannie was a good assistant when it came to babies, but apparently she wasn't as confident with adults, or at least not with this particular adult. Maybe it was a judgment issue.

He tried getting his mind off the man in his truck bed who was cozying up to Fannie. He remembered how she'd once told him her heart was with the little ones. That was one of the times he knew his feelings for her were stronger than he'd expected.

At the hospital he ran inside for a gurney.

He carefully moved Frieda to the stretcher and an orderly helped him push it through the wide doors. Fannie and James followed. Cindy had apparently tired of the company and taken off upon their arrival at the hospital.

"I'd like to see some X-rays," he told the intern. Then he stopped because he knew the Amish had different ways of dealing with health issues, and he didn't want to get in the middle of it.

Fannie lifted her head, ready to speak when James started in again.

"I know Frieda well enough to know she wouldn't want to spend the time and money on this. It'll heal on its own, just like when we bust a leg or something."

Daniel got busy with signing the orders for the tests and tried not to listen to James argue with Fannie.

The next thing he heard was Fannie. "I can't believe you don't trust Daniel."

James smirked. "It's not my family, but I can tell you right here and now, that hip will heal just fine. All this is a waste of money." He huffed out another breath. "I'll get word to Verna."

"The only thing we're wasting is precious time," Fannie said, lifting her shoulders and tilting her chin. She gave the man a look that said she wasn't about to change her mind. Stubborn, that one.

He almost laughed. Cheered. Both.

Daniel stepped up to stand beside her. "Her pain killers will soon wear off. After the tests I'll keep her here in the ER until I hear different."

When Fannie nodded her head, a small smile playing at the corner of her mouth as if digesting their bold move.

"*Danke*," Fannie said to him softly. "For all you did. And do for us."

He took in the word, the one he liked to hear spoken in Dutch. "If you get in any trouble with the bishop, let me know." She looked away when the sound of footsteps approached and stopped at Frieda's cubicle.

Only a couple of minutes had gone by when James came back, clenching his fists. "You be careful now, telling us what needs to be done."

Daniel was surprised to realize that his comment bothered him. James had a point. He couldn't force Frieda or anyone else to do things his way.

Fannie stepped closer and grabbed Daniel's elbow. "You should go, and I should too."

Daniel had rarely seen her want him to leave. It was usually he who had to go.

"Yes, you should." James agreed, giving Fannie a hard stare. "I've arranged for a buggy. I'll drive you home."

"I'm staying with *Mammi*," Fannie said. She motioned with her fingers like she was shooing a fly. "You take the buggy and go."

As he strode away, James muttered toward Daniel, "This isn't your family anymore."

It was late when Daniel was finally able to leave the hospital. The X-rays showed a severe sprain, which was better than the fracture he'd expected to see. He ordered medication for the pain, and saw to it that she was kept comfortable and allowed to rest. At Frieda's age, it was a miracle the bone hadn't broken.

Alone in his car, he had leisure to wait and listen,

although for what he wasn't sure. There were times when he felt a calling from someplace deep in his heart. But it didn't make sense. He'd had a call years ago and left for Mexico to help those who needed medical assistance. Didn't he do his part, make a change?

As he started his car and drove out of the city, past the hustle and bustle of traffic, he found solace. Even if just for a minute, he felt all was well. That was, until he thought of James and the trouble he made.

Daniel wondered if it would be a good idea to keep his distance from Fannie. She was bringing out feelings he hadn't experienced in a long, long time. It was exhilarating and frightening at the same time. Even so, he didn't know if he was ready to let himself feel again. And he didn't want to hurt Fannie.

As he drove up to his house, he noticed Jack's car in front, except it was at an angle instead of against the curb. *What in the world?*

Daniel looked in the window to see Jack asleep in his car. He had known Jack to do some wild things, but he'd never seen him sleep in his car.

His hair was ruffled to one side and appeared to be stuck together like glue. As he got closer the smell of vomit gave him the answer he needed.

Daniel reached into the passenger's door to try and help him out of the car. Jack moaned and his head drooped back to one side.

One eye opened and he tried to focus.

"Jack, I'm taking you inside." Daniel spoke louder than he intended. "You all right down there, Daniel?" An older neighbor called to him from his house across the street.

"I'm fine, thanks." Daniel waved him off. The man was a busybody. More gossip was last thing Daniel needed.

He got Jack to a spare bedroom and plopped him in bed. Tomorrow they would have a long conversation.

Chapter Thirteen

The next morning a groan came from the guestroom. Daniel wanted to groan too. But instead he had to nurse Jack back to his senses.

What a foolish thing to do. Someone needed to intervene, but Daniel wasn't sure he wanted to be that someone. Jack had too many issues in his life that had never been resolved.

He was no psychiatrist but could see his friend's spirit beginning to wither. Knowing this and being able to do something about it were two different things. He usually stayed out of people's lives, but Jack was his friend.

And his friend needed help, especially with his drinking. He hoped Jack would do the right thing so Daniel wouldn't have to intervene. It wouldn't be easy.

By the time Daniel entered his kitchen, Jack was there already. "Where are you off to?" Daniel was honestly surprised Jack was up and dressed.

"Don't you remember me telling you we're on call?"

Daniel frowned and looked at him good and hard. He seemed to be in perfect condition, hair slicked to one side and only slightly wrinkled scrubs.

"You wore those at the club?" Daniel couldn't understand why he was pushing the envelope. He had a lot nerve if he did.

Jack scoffed. "Course not. That would be unethical." His wink and grin said it all, and Daniel was appalled.

"I don't know what's going on, but whatever it is you've got to walk carefully or you're going to lose a lot of good things."

"It's not as bad as you're making it out to be. But if it makes you feel better, I'm working double shifts, so I won't be out on the town any time soon."

"I'm glad to hear that. And I'll hold you to it." Daniel lifted one brow to show Jack he was waiting for that promise to materialize.

Jack help up a hand. "I got it already. I can assure you."

"Good." Daniel didn't like playing big brother, but that was how it seemed to be lately and it made him wonder.

Jack came from a well-to-do family. Medical school and residency pressure was hard enough to go through without family issues as well.

"Hey, if you want to help me out on any of the deliveries, let me know. I know you thought about obstetrics."

Jack snorted and stood tall, as if showing Daniel he was fine. "Enough already."

Daniel's phone vibrated, and he checked the ID. Cindy.

The dinner date they'd planned came to him. He panicked, wondering if he'd missed it.

"You at the hospital?" He hoped she was but wasn't sure why.

"Yes, where are you?" Her voice held an even tone,

which he took as meaning he hadn't forgotten anything. Then he remembered. Dinner tonight.

"I'm on my way to the Amish for the morning. I'll be back for the evening shift. Will you be around…for dinner tonight?" Now he hoped she'd say yes, surprising himself. She was the first woman he'd dated since Emily died, and he'd had a nice time at Sergio's. It had been far too long.

"Sure, I'll be around."

"Good." He still felt awkward and wasn't sure what to say so he decided to change the subject. "How is Frieda doing?"

"She's being released this morning." Cindy spoke professionally.

He pointed to Jack, letting him know he was watching him. And he would be. He motioned to his car, and Jack followed him.

"Daniel, is there someone there with you?"

"As a matter of fact, Jack. And he needs a day off.

"Oh, well I'll let you go then." Her irritation oozed through the phone, but Daniel was stuck between them.

"So, dinner?"

He heard a sigh. "Yes, in the cafeteria. See you at work."

Daniel dropped the phone and listened to Jack gripe all the way to his car.

"You're giving me a day off? I don't think the chief of staff will appreciate me not showing up." He opened the driver's side door and crawled in.

"You need one."

"I hate to admit you're right, but this time you are."

He stuck out his hand, and Daniel shook it. A minute later Jack pulled away from the curb.

As Daniel drove to the community, he decided to stop by the Amish pastry shop where Fannie worked when they needed extra help.

The smell of fresh rolls and danishes along with a strong cup of coffee sounded great at the moment. But as he drove closer, he could see a line of customers snaking out the door. Disappointed, he decided to pass. He was late already.

The sunrise always seemed to bring out feelings of missing the community. This morning was no different. Nothing seemed to change. The sight of crops flowing in the wind or the sounds of creaking buggies brought him back every time. And he was home again.

Leaving was a difficult decision. The bishop was dead set against it because he was sure Daniel wouldn't come back. Maybe his medical considerations would come to light one of these years.

As he got closer to Fannie's *haus*, a group of children noticed him and started running to him.

"*Ach*, it's the new doc!" a little red-haired boy called out.

Another almost caught up with his truck. He slowed down, and they circled around him.

"Are you going to help *Mammi* Hochstetler?

They continued to follow him, asking questions as they went.

He wanted to stop and answer, but there were so many questions, he couldn't even hear each one much less answer them.

"I'm going to check on things now," he said to the little boy.

By the time he got to their home, he was telling himself to think the best not the worst, a simple but comforting phrase his professor told him.

"What in the world is going on here?" Verna answered his knock and watched the swarm of children at their door.

Daniel shrugged. "I'm not sure, but I would like to see Fannie. Is she here?"

"She's at the pastry shop this morning. She called a neighbor to bring a buggy early this morning. *Mammi* was released, and she brought her home."

Daniel managed to maneuver around the little ones. "Why are there so many kids around?"

They surged past him and into the house.

"They're waiting for Fannie too." Verna smiled.

Frieda sat comfortably on the sofa, patting the children's cheeks as they scrambled to sit beside her, while Daniel tried to find a way through.

"Careful there, kids," Daniel called as soon as he stepped inside. "Her hip is still healing."

Frieda waved a hand at him, shooing away his concern. She enjoyed having the children around, even if they weren't really there to see her.

"Well, look who's here." Fannie stood in the door, chuckling. "What in the world is going on in here?"

Daniel dashed for the door and let himself breathe. "Why are they so exited?"

She smiled at the children, who were still squirreling

about and laughing. Then she gazed at him, her smile a bit more flirtatious than he'd seen before.

He squinted and waited, thinking. "Ah. So that's why they were chasing me," he said as she pulled out a bag of cookies and pastries.

"I brought some home with me."

She smiled. "I enjoy baking. They asked me to work there more days, and I said yes."

Daniel frowned as a little one ran behind him. He pulled up a chair and sat. "Will you still have time to do everything?

"You mean help with the deliveries? Of course."

"Are you sure? It's just going to get even more hectic."

"Have you changed your mind? About my being your midwife, I mean?"

"Not at all. I just don't want to overwhelm you. You'll have two jobs and the care of this house. And the three of you are alone." He sighed. Nothing like stating the obvious. But her expression said she understood. He meant they didn't have a man around to help them.

The children had been given their cookies and began to file out. The house quieted as they left.

"So, what's on for the schedule today?" Fannie asked.

"Wait for another delivery and check on Frieda." Daniel stood and went over to examine her. "How's the hip?"

She winced a bit while he checked her hip, but seemed to be okay. "So will I live?"

He patted her hand. "It may take a while for the pain to completely go away. But it's my professional opinion that you will be just fine. You're fortunate it wasn't worse."

He gave her instructions about activities she could

and couldn't do and reminded her of the importance of moving around to keep from getting stiff. "So take care not to just play Queen Bee and let Fannie and Verna wait on you hand and foot." He laughed. "You need to be upright as much as possible. "

She laughed, and as he closed his bag, she said, "Thanks, Doc."

They both grinned a little, as that title was for the community doctor, not Daniel.

Chapter Fourteen

Just keep the babe comfortable. I'm almost done." Daniel wasn't surprised that Fannie did so well handling the newborns. It had been just over a week since she'd delivered the Lapps' newest little one almost on her own. If he read her right, she was as proud as the new *mamm*.

"She's beautiful." Fannie hadn't taken her hands off the baby since Daniel had finished her checkup.

He decided that when they left the house in a bit, he would tell her not to get so attached. He understood why she did, but it didn't set well with his work.

"Time to clean up," he said, hoping to move her attention from the baby.

She turned to him and held the baby a little tighter. "It feels like we just got here."

"She and her mother are both doing well, thanks in part to you. You should be pleased." Fannie was improving with every delivery. He felt confident she would be a good midwife.

And a good wife. He jolted. Where had that come?

"Penny for your thoughts?" She smiled.

When she looked at him like that, he let his guard down a little and acknowledged that they were a good team. But that was all they could be. He waited for Emily's image to flit into his mind, but it didn't come.

He shook his head, as if he could rid it of unwanted—no, unexpected—thoughts. "You should take a day off," he said to Fannie. "Spend time with Frieda."

"And leave you to take on all of these babies?" She was rocking the baby again, which made him smile.

"You've got a point. Can you give her up so I can go to the hospital?" He had to admit, he didn't want to leave either. Because of Fannie, he was finding it hard to leave the community and return to his other world. "We both have work to do. Are you working at the bakery today?"

"*Jah*, I suppose I should be going." Fannie sighed and handed the babe over to her *mamm*. "I'll check on some tea for you." She disappeared out the door.

"Dr. Kauffman, *danke*." Mrs. Lapp looked down at her newborn child then up at Daniel. "I'll be paying you soon." She shook a finger at him as if she wouldn't accept any objections.

"I remember you make a good pecan pie." Daniel lifted his forehead as he waited for the answer and found himself hungry just thinking about it.

"I'll make you two for good measure." The beaming mother lowered her eyes back to her baby as if it was her first, even though she had four others to tend to.

Amish let nature decide the number of their families. God was in charge in every aspect of their lives. He especially admired this practice when it came to those who were more liberal about the choice a woman makes to have a child. Yet, still, he did not judge.

One of Mrs. Lapp's other children watched as he gathered up his instruments. A little girl who could barely see over the bedside table watched as he sanitized each tool.

"What's that?" another asked as she pointed to the stethoscope. It was then Daniel decided that whoever said children should be seen and not heard was on to something.

"Let the doctor work now," their mother told them. "Sorry, Dr. Kauffman. You shoo them away if you need to." She looked back down at the tiny bundle in her arms.

"Even after all the children you've had, you're treating this one as if it's your first. I imagine you've been that way with each." He couldn't even imagine one child, let alone this brood.

Once packed up, he glanced around the room to make sure he had everything and then made his way out of the house.

"*Danke*, Doctor, for checking in on the babe." Mr. Lapp beamed with pride as he stuck a pipe that held no tobacco between his teeth, as was the Amish way.

Daniel smiled as he shook the man's hand and made his way out. He enjoyed watching the Lapps dote on their new arrival even with so many children already underfoot. He called good-bye to Fannie as he left the house. She would stay a while longer.

As he walked toward his truck, he heard a sound. The chickens were squawking and the cattle mooing. Was there a coyote or some other animal in the area?

He wasn't a big hunter, but he thought again that working in the country may be one of the times he should carry a gun.

He was just about to his truck when the animals started to calm down, which created even more curiosity. He followed the sounds until they slowly disappeared near the back of the barn.

The place was filled with bales of hay and stalls for milking. Cats ran at the sight of him, and he saw what he least expected.

"It's okay. I'm a doctor." When he didn't hear a response, he repeated it in Pennsylvania Dutch. He stood stock still. A little blonde girl backed herself into a corner, trembling, with dirty drips of water falling down her cheeks.

He held out his hand. She made her way to Daniel, tiny steps of reluctance led to desperation, and she looked as though she hadn't eaten in far too long.

She stopped and stared at him, and he mimicked her actions, slowly.

Daniel felt a lump in his throat, something he hadn't felt for a long while. He'd always enjoyed seeing the children in their attire, and the little ones like this one always got the best of him.

He bent over so as not to look down at her. When he got closer he could see bright green eyes, the same as Fannie's.

"You help your folks out with your new sister, all right?"

She shook her head and held out her Amish doll. The tattered shreds of what was left of it made him want to go right back to the house and give her a new one.

Daniel hadn't noticed dirt on the faces of the children he'd just seen in the house, nor did any of the girls have soiled dresses.

He paused. "What's your doll's name?"

She didn't respond, and Daniel became uneasy and decided to turn the conversation over to her *daed*. He kneeled and tried to get her to tell him her name, to take him to her house—if she lived there at all. She sat down but didn't reply.

He stood and when he did she immediately did too. She looked over at the big house and pointed to herself. It made no sense.

Daniel led her to the house and tried to hold her hand, but her fearful eyes told him the answer was no.

Chapter Fifteen

After making Mrs. Lapp some tea and being sure the new babe had been suckling properly, Fannie hurried out the door.

Daniel called to her from near his truck. She looked up in surprise, certain he'd left ten minutes ago.

She made her way to him. He stood between the barn and his truck, a young girl at his side.

"What's this?" She crouched down by the girl. "Who are you?"

The girl shrank behind Daniel's legs.

"I'm glad you're here." Daniel wore a face she'd never seen on him and knew this was no ordinary situation.

Fannie stood to look at Daniel. "Who is she? Where did she come from?"

"She was in the barn. I presume she lives here. But she doesn't want to go in, and I didn't want to make her."

Fannie glanced at the girl but wasn't surprised that she quickly looked downward.

"I see." Although, truth be told, she really didn't. Fannie slowly knelt but when she looked her in the eyes, the young girl shifted her eyes away again. "We shouldn't talk about her like this."

"Talk to her instead," Daniel said.

Fannie nodded in agreement. "My name is Fannie. If you want to tell me your name, maybe we can talk."

The girl's eyes widened as if she wanted to but couldn't get her voice to go past her chest.

"Does anyone know where you are?" Fannie prayed for an answer.

The girl stared at her.

Fannie straightened up. "Let's ask the family. We'll feel pretty silly if she is one of theirs and was just off playing with her doll in the barn."

They made their way back to the *haus*.

"Have you heard her speak?"

Daniel reached for Fannie. "Slow down. I tried to take her to the door, but she was too scared to go in the house. That's all I know."

The front door opened and a younger girl—Miriam, Fannie thought—walked out and made her way to the girl, ignoring Fannie and Daniel. The child stood still, but when she saw that it was a young girl who opened the door she seemed to breathe a little easier.

"Hi, Dr. Kauffman. Who's this?" Miriam was full of curiosity.

Fannie's heart skipped. "You don't know her?"

She shook her head. "*Nee*, but she can stay with us."

Daniel winked. "No worries." He turned aside to Fannie and whispered, "I'll talk to them." He moved forward to walk the girl to the door.

But before they could approach, Mr. Lapp stepped

out. He handed Daniel a wad of money and pumped his hand. "I'm glad you're still here. For the delivery."

"Was this one the last before today's?" He looked over at the child. "I found her in your barn."

Mr. Lapp's eyes widened. "Ah, no. I can't say as we're acquainted."

"So you don't know this girl?" Daniel asked one last time.

"*Nee*, but since you ask…I've noticed some seed missing in the barn. I figured the mice or birds got into it."

"You think she ate seed?" It seemed unbelievable. "I can't imagine…where did you get this idea?" Fannie asked.

He sighed deeply before answering. "I can think of no other explanation. If you saw her in the barn…" He looked around to see if anyone was listening.

She glanced at him and then quickly looked away.

"I hate to think why she's here." Mr. Lapp looked at the little girl and seemed to have the same reaction they'd all had. "I'll make a call at the community phone and let you know if anything comes up."

Unease filled his eyes as he turned and jogged down the lane.

Fannie turned her gaze on the young girl. What would she be doing out here on her own? She was obviously Amish by her dress. But Fannie wondered about that too. Amish dresses are made and sold in the local shops without a question. Anyone could wear one and hope they'd be thought to belong in the community.

"What would keep her from communicating with us and cause her to be so timid?

Daniel glanced over at the child. Fannie followed

his gaze, assuming the girl couldn't hear what they were saying since they kept their voices low. The girl and Miriam squatted in the dirt, more than a few feet away but still in earshot if they spoke up.

"I wonder what our place is in this situation. Do we share this with only those here today until Mr. Lapp gets back with some news?" Fannie asked.

"If there is someone around who would have some ulterior motive concerning this child, we need her to be under lock and key until we see how she managed to end up here alone—eating seed to survive—and where her family might be and if it's safe for her to go—" Fannie stopped to take a breath.

"Fannie, do you realize how you're dealing with this?" Daniel scanned her face, searching for something. "Too much, too quick. Let's take it one thing at a time."

Her first thought was he was being his usual rational self, but she had a feeling he was invested in this situation as well. The glances he kept shooting at the girl told on him.

Perhaps it was time to test his commitment to her and to the community. "Okay then, where is she going to stay?"

"I assumed with the Lapps. She's already got a friend in Miriam. Or you, just until we can canvas the community for information."

The way he said that made her feel a pang in her chest. She was told she'd never have a child due to health complications. It just wasn't meant to be. But the natural desire to be a *mamm* was still upon her.

"Fannie, are you with me?" Daniel's voice brought her back, and she gazed lovingly at the child.

"*Jah*, I want to take her. She's been around enough strange people without more to meet."

He smirked.

She put a fist on her hip. "You were expecting that, weren't you?"

"She would be in good hands, and so would you."

Sometimes she thought he knew what she was thinking before she said it.

As they turned to watch the girls playing, they both stopped when they saw the girls sitting in the grass, picking dandelions.

"They seem to have the system down." Fannie smiled.

Daniel grinned a little as he watched the girls collect the yellow blooms into large bunches.

Their ingenuity fascinated Fannie, and she tried to figure out what the finishing touch would be.

"You look like you'd like to be in there with them." Daniel's deep voice was enough to spur her on to go sit with Miriam and the little one they'd just met.

Before she did, she wondered what to call her. "What should I say?"

"You don't need to say anything. Just be there with her."

He seemed to be as vested in this as she was. But then who wouldn't be with what she seemed to have gone through? The thought of the little blonde child hiding in the Lapp barn for who knew how long, eating seed to survive—Fannie shuddered.

"May I join you?" Fannie approached the pair and immediately noticed Miriam picking her own stash of dandelions. The little girl stood and watched.

Fannie picked a couple more blooms and handed

them to the girl, but she thrust her hands behind her and wouldn't accept them.

Mr. Lapp came into view up the dirt road. Miriam ran up to him. As he approached Fannie and Daniel, he shook his head. "There's no missing child alert."

Chapter Sixteen

"So, what's next?" Daniel and Fannie exchanged worried glances, and then looked back to Mr. Lapp.

"The police will investigate even without a report. They weren't certain how soon. Meantime she needs to be comforted."

They certainly couldn't just sit and wait for the police investigation before intervening. Whatever pain the child felt in her world right now was shaking Daniel up as well.

"It's hard to know what to do," Mr. Lapp said. "But I have an idea where to start." He turned to his daughter. "How about if you get in the tub? And get started washing those clothes."

His belly laugh garnered both girls' attention. He pointed to the river. Miriam spared no time rushing into the nearby river alongside the house.

Daniel glanced at his watch. He needed to head back to the hospital but didn't want to leave.

He'd recently had less interest in his rotation at the hospital, switching shifts more often than he should. He hadn't been so irresponsible since…since Emily's death.

He told himself it was because of the increased number of expectant mothers this spring. But a secret part of his heart knew he was intrigued with the community and with Fannie.

He also had to admit he enjoyed being the hero who was fortunate enough to be the first to bring a little person into the world.

Fannie and Daniel chuckled as the girl's eyes lit up. But something stopped her from following Miriam. She just stood still and watched Miriam run to the water and jump in.

Mrs. Lapp appeared on the front porch, dressed and in her *kapp* and holding the newborn. She approached her husband, handed him the babe, and then walked over to the young girl and took her hand. "Baby steps. That's all you need child, one step at a time."

Three other girls materialized on the path. When they saw their *mamm* urging the girl to follow Miriam, they rushed past them to the water, soon squealing and splashing. They called to Mrs. Lapp and her new charge to join them.

"Still not a word or touch from her." Daniel spoke so quietly he wasn't sure that Fannie heard him.

But when she turned to him, her expression seemed filled with the same sadness he felt at the little girl's plight, perhaps something even deeper.

Mr. Lapp stepped up. "Yours was probably the first kind face she's seen for a while. She'll need you around. I hope you can stop by again."

Daniel nodded. "I will when I can."

A few minutes later Mrs. Lapp headed up the bank from the creek, holding the little girl's hand. Two very wet and shivering Lapp daughters trailed behind, chattering and laughing. But it was the solemn child who again captured Daniel's attention.

Mrs. Lapp walked over to her husband and gathered the newborn into her. She looked down at the upturned face of the child. "We'll take good care of her."

"I know she'll be in excellent hands." That he was sure of.

"Stop by tomorrow, if you're making rounds." Mrs. Lapp looked Daniel in the eyes, and he nodded gratefully.

Fannie was disappointed the girl wouldn't be going with her, but this seemed best for now.

As Daniel and Fannie climbed into the pickup, he said, "I know why you've spent more time here today, but you don't seem to be in any hurry to get home. Something going on there, I mean besides your grandmother's fall?"

She laughed lightly. "Honestly, sometimes they wear me out. They try my patience with their arguing and sharp opinions." She let out a breath. "It's easier to be with each alone, but even then they're quite... a handful."

"They're opinionated," he said, laughing with her. "That can be entertaining once in a while, but I can only imagine what it's like to live with them."

He stopped at the fork in the road. It had been a long day for them both, but even so he didn't want it to end. The little girl was in his thoughts, and the reality of the woman beside him, the thought of her getting out of the truck and walking away from him, made the hours left in the day seem bleak.

Fannie was studying him. "Penny for your thoughts."

He tried to think of something clever to say, something to make her stay. He didn't want to be alone. He realized that hadn't happened in a very long time. "Here." He pulled a penny from his pocket. "You first."

She smiled and turned a little closer to him. She drew a deep breath before speaking. "I have to say...you never talk about anyone. I go home to *Mamm* and *Mammi*, but you...you haven't spoken about anyone since we started working together."

He managed to keep his voice even. "Except Emily."

"Yes, Emily. What a pretty name."

He shook his head. "That was years ago. But even before she passed away, our home life was becoming strained."

"You two weren't happily married?" she asked just above a whisper.

"I thought so. But...looking back on it now, I sometimes wonder why we did it, got married so young."

She glanced at him, curiosity on her face. "And have you decided?"

"Not really. We believed we were in love. It seemed like the logical thing. I wasn't raised to live with a girl without being married. But I was always at the hospital, and she was bored with her job and being home alone all the time. I think she was getting ready to leave me before the accident."

"I'm sorry."

He shrugged. "It was a long time ago. Sometimes things don't work out the way you expect."

She nodded. "Like the first time I declined a proposal. I left on my own accord."

"Do you regret it now?"

She shifted in her seat, considering. She shook her head. "I'm too independent. My *daed* was happy letting

Mamm make all the decisions, but most men want someone obedient. I'm not sure I can just be quiet and obey."

"Is that really how you see marriage, that someone has to be in charge of running the other person?"

She rubbed the back of her neck. "I didn't think of it that way, but I suppose so."

"No, Fannie. Marriage is give and take, two people working together. Sometimes one gives in on a subject, but the next time the other does. Marriage is not a dictatorship."

Her brow furrowed. "But your parents—"

"Not a good example. My *daed* taught me what not to do, how not to treat my wife. I learned well. From Emily, I learned how a woman should be cared for. I failed her, but I did learn the lesson."

They both stopped talking and let the stillness seep in, and for a time they were silent.

"I'd best get you home." He pressed the accelerator, ending their conversation

Chapter Seventeen

Daniel stood at the nurses' station going over his charts. But he found it hard to concentrate. His mind was elsewhere, something that seemed to be happening more often now.

A day without Fannie was too long. And now, even each hour that passed when he couldn't be with the Amish, or with her, seemed to drag. He had to face it: she had taken up residence in his heart.

The lost child was probably taking up what extra time she had, which he completely understood. But a phone call would have been nice if she'd been allowed to use the community phone.

"Hey, Daniel."

He turned to see Jack heading toward him at a hurried clip. "Sorry, I was distracted."

Jack grunted. "With the Amish again?"

Daniel didn't like the way Jack said their name. It bugged him more than usual anyway. At least Cindy was respectful about his heritage. There seemed to be two kinds of outsiders: those who were fascinated with the

Amish way of life and those who thought them weak and strange.

"I don't appreciate your inflection," Daniel said.

"Sorry, I didn't know you were so sensitive." Jack's voice cut between him and his thoughts of Fannie.

"Sorry, Jack. I've just got a lot on my mind." He paused then changed the subject. "You feeling better than the last time I saw you?" Should he have brought it up? Probably not, but it was too late.

"Why do you ask...Oh yeah. You still thinking about that?"

"Well, yeah. It's not every day you end up crashing at my place."

But Jack was obviously not finished with the Amish question. "So what is it that keeps pulling you out there?"

Jack's question echoed his own thoughts. He was more surprised than anyone that he was being pulled back. When he left the community, he had not planned on going back. Now, while he made his rounds at the hospital, all he could thing about were his Amish patients. And Fannie. But when he was in the community, drinking coffee with a *daed* after a delivery, he couldn't wait to get back to the hospital.

"Are these Amish getting to you? Do you think you're better than the rest of us?" Jack's voice was too loud, ringing out in the quiet hallway and completely unnecessary.

Daniel cut him a look. "Better than the rest of who?"

"Other doctors who have to cover for you when you're on call." He paused, pointing at himself with his thumb. "Namely, *moi*."

"Daniel, Jack, come into my office." The chief of staff

rounded a corner where he must have heard everything. He strode down the hall. Daniel and Jack followed like two abashed boys, being scolded for fighting on the playground.

The chief sat at this desk and looked from one to the other. "I'm not sure what's going between the two of you, but whatever that is, fix it. If I notice something is off, so will your patients. Now go and do your jobs."

They both stood to leave, but the chief called Daniel back before he reached the door.

Daniel returned slowly.

"Take a seat." Dr. Ambrose twined his fingers and waited for Daniel to follow sit. "I understand you are spending more hours with the Amish community than planned."

Daniel nodded. "Yes, though I mentioned the possibility in my last report."

"Yes, I remember. But now my concern is the issue between you and Jack, your on-call commitment, the hours you owe the hospital, the hours you owe your colleagues—no matter how good the reason you're otherwise occupied. "

Dr. Ambrose was right. He had no excuse.

"I've heard you're helping out at some sort of community clinic." He twined his fingers and looked at Daniel long and hard. "You're a good man, Daniel, and a good doctor. I don't want to lose you, but if this community continues to exert its pull on you, away from your responsibilities here, our next discussion will need to clarify your priorities and future plans." He didn't come right out and say so, but Daniel knew he meant his contract with the hospital would be broken.

"I understand. I hope to work at the clinic only a few hours each week. There's a community midwife who's turned into quite a capable nurse. She'll be in charge of the clinic." He hoped.

The chief changed the subject then to the Cavaliers' chances in the playoffs. Daniel made small talk about sports while his mind reeled with the implications of Dr. Ambrose's pointed words.

After saying good-bye, Daniel returned to the nurses' station.

The one thing that stuck in his brain was juggling his time between the Amish and the hospital. There was much truth in the chief's concerns. Maybe he needed to decide which was more important during the season. He shook his head. Between Fannie and the young Amish girl, his thoughts were elsewhere.

"Where were you just now?" Cindy stood beside him, only inches away but he hadn't noticed her approach.

"Oh, hey. I was talking to the man in charge." He hiked a thumb over his shoulder.

Her brow furrowed, and she paused for a moment. "Is everything okay?"

"I'm not sure." He didn't want to get into it, but his demeanor must have shown something was wrong, given Cindy's reaction.

"Want to grab some coffee?" She seemed sincere but there was something in her expression that made him uncomfortable. "And talk?"

"I've got too much to do."

She let out a loud sigh. "I can see why you haven't asked me to dinner lately. Too busy." Her tone was light, flirtatious, but the way she looked at him was dead serious. And a clear attempt to make him feel guilty. He wondered if she imagined there was an understanding of some kind between them.

Again, that uncomfortable feeling swept over him. He wouldn't allow himself to get sucked into the guilt trip. He had good reason to help his people.

It took great effort to keep the irritation out of his voice. "Yeah, the needs in the community take precedence this time of year." He raised a brow, challenging her to disagree. She was a nurse. As a health professional, at the very least, she should understand the Hippocratic Oath.

She laughed, easing the moment of tension between them. "Sounds like our date may have to consist of me helping you deliver a baby." She grinned at him and lifted her brow, waiting for his response.

"I'll let you know if I need another hand."

Fannie and Cindy working with him in the same room? He almost laughed. "It's not the same there as it is here. You understand."

His mind drifted back to the community, to the little girl with no words. She was in good hands with a great family. But something about her nagged at the edges of his mind. He couldn't place what it was; the answer remained just out of reach.

"Daniel!" Cindy's voice rang in his ear and brought him back to the moment. Then he heard the page.

"Sorry. I have a patient to tend to. We'll talk soon." He touched her shoulder and, without waiting for her to reply, walked away.

The next hours passed in a blur of patients and rounds and talking with nurses and aides. Finally he shucked his lab coat and prepared for the rest of his day in Amish country.

He drove through the countryside of spring colors and roadside stands full of early vegetables. As always, he had the urge to pull over, enjoy the sights and smells of nature's bounty, and pick up a few vegetables. But given his busy schedule, he seldom had the time to prepare a meal.

Pastries on the other hand...he grinned...they'd not go to waste. Neither would the homemade chocolates. He could almost taste them as he pulled over at the next roadside stand. Talk about temptation.

But even more tempting, the chocolate would give him another a reason to see Fannie.

Chapter Eighteen

"What were you thinking? I can't do all of this. I'm a midwife. I'm supposed to help with *mamms* and babies, not sick folks." Fannie glanced around the small waiting room then back to Daniel, her eyebrows raised.

Daniel's work with the deliveries made him popular in the community. Now people were coming to him for other kinds of medical needs, so many that he was spending more time at the clinic Doc Reuben let him set up in town.

He grinned at Fannie, which stopped her in her tracks. "We'll talk later," he said. "You're doing a fine job. And besides, your first patient is here." He inclined his head toward Almina Helmuth, very large with child, who'd just waddled through the doorway, a little girl holding on to her skirt.

"I haven't seen you for ages. Now I see why." Fannie looked Almina up and down and smiled. Once the woman started talking, there was no stopping her.

"I'm tired. Can't be as active as I need to be for this one. She needs a playmate." Almina smiled. "Let me put it this way, I'm the one who needs her to find a playmate." She chuckled and patted her stomach. "So I can sit down and rest." The *mamm* looked down at her daughter.

Fannie sympathized.

Mrs. Helmuth hurried on. "I heard about the little girl who doesn't speak, the one they've started calling Lydia. Anyway, I heard she's been staying with the Hershbergers while the Lapps have family visiting. I sent a message to Alina Hershberger letting her know I'd be here around this time. Said I thought the little girls might like to play during my time with the doctor. She sent word back that she'd try to make it and bring the poor little girl with her. But she's not here yet, is she? As for what the bishop plans to do about the girl, now that's another story. He says he needs time to sort things out. But she—the little girl, I'm talking about—didn't come out of nowhere, if you ask me. The bishop also said that—" She paused to catch her breath.

"As long as she's safe," Fannie broke in. "That's what counts."

"Yes, but what a terrible thing. Who would just go off and leave a little child on her own that way? Okay, now then, I'm ready to see the doctor. I'm exhausted." She walked heavily over to Daniel's examination room. From the sound of his murmurs and her replies, she had gained too much weight, and she wasn't happy about it.

The bell over the door rang as another patient, a local farmer, walked in. Fannie looked up from the counter. "Jeremy. I haven't seen you around."

"*Ach*, Fannie. Been trying to heal this thing, but I don't think it's gonna get better."

He unwrapped a handkerchief from his hand. His thumb oozed yellow infection.

She fought to keep from turning away from the discolored finger. "Jeremy, how long ago did this happen?"

"A while ago. It's coming on planting season. I can't be laid up getting something like this fixed."

"If you don't get it taken care of, you're going to miss more than a finger." She led him to a treatment room and began cleaning the wound.

She looked up to see Daniel grinning at her in the doorway.

"Fannie, swab it, stick the sample in a bag so we can test it, and then clean up the infected area. Penicillin should be somewhere around here."

"What happened to the babies?" She gathered what he needed. "I didn't sign up for these extras."

"Doc Reuben's not in town." Daniel lifted his brow, which seemed to mean they were switching gears. "We may get some deliveries."

She sighed. "Okay, then. I'll be prepared for both."

"Good thinking." He winked, which made her insides freeze.

Lately she worried about being alone with him. They'd gotten to know each other better, but that didn't mean anything had changed. They still irritated each other. She tried to hold on to that thought while her insides settled back to normal.

"Fannie, are you with me?" He'd been watching her, which made her cheeks warm.

"What does penicillin do?" She already knew, but it was the first thing that popped into her head. She almost needed to fan her face.

"It does away with the bad bacteria in your body, keeps the germs at bay. Good of you to ask. I'll take a look at it."

As he examined Jeremy's finger, the bell chimed over the door.

Fannie hurried back to the waiting room just as Mrs. Hershberger entered with the child Almina said was now called Lydia.

Fannie crouched down. "*Hallo,*" she said softly.

"I heard Almina Helmuth was looking for a playmate for her daughter." Mrs. Hershberger folded her arms. "We thought we'd give them a few minutes to play together."

Lydia stood by, her eyes large, seeming to take in everything and everyone. Fannie wondered again if she couldn't speak or if she didn't want to. "Almina's just finished being examined by Dr. Kauffman. Here's her daughter." Fannie indicated the quiet girl still waiting in one of the straight-back wooden chairs.

Fannie bent down next to Lydia and tried to read how she might be feeling. "Will you tell me if you're okay or if you're not?"

Lydia looked around the room. Her eyes lit on the Helmuth girl and her gaze turned to longing.

"It's okay to play with her," Fannie said. "Just stay close."

Still no response.

Fannie breathed a quick prayer for this girl and for guidance as to what and how much they should do for her.

Fannie had no problem staying by her side for as long as needed. But she hurt for the young girl. And she didn't want to get too attached.

She saw how that could easily happen. Each time Lydia looked at her with her big green eyes, so much like her own, her heart melted.

Lydia sat by the Helmuth child, and they played with their dolls, side by side. Lydia's doll was not quite as dirty as it had been when Fannie first saw her. Perhaps Mrs. Lapp or Mrs. Hershberger had convinced the girl to let them give the doll a bath.

Strangely, though, Lydia seemed to prefer Fannie's company. Even before Almina Helmuth left with her daughter, Lydia had become Fannie's little blonde shadow. Fannie and Mrs. Hershberger exchanged glances. It was the first intentional interaction either had observed in the child.

"Will you let her stay a few minutes?" Fannie asked as Mrs. Hershberger started getting ready to leave.

"Of course," she said. "Maybe we can break through that silent wall yet." She turned at the door and blew a kiss to Lydia.

When Lydia wasn't with Fannie, she was one step behind Daniel.

Fannie took in Lydia's oversized dress. Perhaps that was the only one Mrs. Hershberger could find. But with all the children in the community, surely someone could come up with a dress that fit her.

A voice floated out of the examining room where Daniel was treating a burn wound. "*Jah* know I could just get some kerosene and put it in a can. That would get things done real quick."

Daniel spoke mildly. "That's not a good idea. It would just lead to more difficulties."

Fannie went to the open doorway and watched Daniel gently covering Jeremy's wound with salve. "Better?"

The young man lifted his nose. "*Nee*, not really. But as long as it clears up, I guess I'm all right."

"You'll be fine." He turned and went over to Lydia.

Fannie watched as he spoke to her, softly, in her ear.

She was curious as to what he was saying and a bit surprised that Lydia looked at him, making eye contact. Another big step forward.

He led the child back to his work area. Daniel pointed at his finger, at hers, then continued walking. Her tiny fingers were too small for her to clasp any of Daniel's except for his little finger.

When he looked up, his eyes met Fannie's, and she smiled.

The door chimed, and a woman came in with a cane that catered to her left leg. "Is Dr. Kauffman in?" A man, most likely her husband, held the door for her.

Once inside she limped to a chair. He followed, looking like he could barely stand upright.

"*Jah*, take a seat, and I'll fetch him for you."

As she walked to his office, she realized he was going to end up doing a little bit of everything. All kinds of doctoring. She wasn't sure about that and decided she'd talk to him about it at the end of the day.

"You got the *Farm and Ranch Catalogue*?" the husband asked Fannie when she walked back into the room with Lydia in tow.

"I believe so. If not, the *Budget* came this morning." She smiled to keep his spirits up. "How are you?" He was in obvious pain but seemed to be trying to stay strong.

"We're both in bad shape." He frowned. "She twisted

her ankle, and I've got an upset stomach and fever. And we've got family on the way to visit."

Fannie went to the back and filled a cup with water for the woman.

"I thought you might like something cold to drink." The woman's hand shook but accepted the cup. "*Danke.*"

"Our children and their families are coming up from Virginia." She cringed but went on. "I just hope this won't keep me from too much. Do you think a boot will be enough?"

Fannie shook her head. "I can't tell you, but you seem to be in a lot of pain so I wouldn't push it too much." The door opened again and another woman entered. A teenager followed her, then an elderly man. They all took seats and ignored each other. The waiting room suddenly became too noisy, too crowded. Voices rose, two above the others…

"That's what I've been telling her," said the husband of the woman with the twisted ankle. His face was pale, his forehead beaded with sweat. "But no, she doesn't listen." He shifted on his chair, scowling at his wife.

Fannie realized she was about to be pulled into a marital disagreement and needed to get out.

"You let me know if you need anything." She took Lydia's hand and started to walk away.

The woman looked at Lydia and spoke softly. "*Hallo*, little one."

Lydia looked away and held tight to Fannie's hand.

Daniel stepped into the anteroom. "Is everything all right?"

The arguing stopped, and the room fell silent. Fannie drew in a deep breath. "It is now."

She scanned the small waiting room, her gaze lingering on the faces of young and old, the injured, the sick, the expectant mothers.

She glanced at Daniel, taking in the compassion she saw in his face. She blinked and looked again.

Compassion. That's why he worked so hard in the community, even after putting in so many hours at the hospital.

Tears stung her eyes, and she blinked rapidly.

When it came down to it, that's why she had chosen to become a midwife. Yet it seemed that God was stretching her view of her world and of herself.

She felt someone's gaze on her and looked down. Lydia's face was tilted up, and for just a tiny second Fannie thought the child might smile.

Her heart warmed.

The full noisy waiting room seemed to fade. The only thing that mattered was that little girl's smile.

Fannie stooped down and took her hand, and holding it gently, she smiled into her eyes.

Daniel pulled a chair over and sat. Their eyes met over the top of the child's eyes.

It seemed as if the world stopped spinning. Before she could react, someone in the waiting room grumbled about the doctor taking too long.

With a good-natured grin, Daniel stood and walked into the waiting room. "Who's next?"

The couple who'd spent the last several minutes arguing grumbled past Fannie and Lydia. Daniel winked again as he passed her.

Fannie grinned. Had Daniel changed? Or had she?

A slight stirring caught her attention. With wonder she watched Lydia trying to wink at her tattered doll.

Chapter Nineteen

A few days later Daniel stood in the clinic waiting room, watching the rain come down in sheets. The weather would keep many patients away. He knew it wouldn't keep Fannie away and sure enough, here she came, hurrying down the street toward the clinic, clutching an umbrella and a paper sack.

"Wouldn't you know, the day we're ready for a rush and it rains cats and dogs?" Fannie set her bag on the desk and tucked her hair under her *kapp*. "You're here today, so of course there will be no babies. They only like to come when you're tired after working at the hospital or have been up all night. Let me guess—you got a good night's sleep last night."

"I did. Like the rain, it ebbs and flows. You can't control Mother Nature for either new babes or rainstorms." Daniel hadn't realized how much she liked doing deliveries until this conversation.

"Well, I hope it passes sooner rather than later. I have too much time on my hands." She scanned the room and then looked back at him. A few mothers-to-be had braved the storm to visit the clinic. He'd already seen them all and given them a clean bill of health. The four women had decided to sit until the weather cleared enough for them to walk home without drowning.

"Lydia's here?" She nodded to the young girl sitting near the clutch of *mamms*, not a part of them yet not far away either.

"Mrs. Hershberger brought her by. She thought perhaps a patient coming through would recognize her."

"And?"

"No one seems to know her."

"Mind if I mingle a little?" Fannie lifted her brow in question.

"Not at all. I have some charting to do. But keep an eye out for the mail."

"Something important?"

"Medical supplies. So I guess that would be a yes." He smiled and she did too.

As he watched Fannie chat with a mother-to-be, he noticed her touches. A hand on her shoulder, a smile, or listening ear. Although she had never gone through school to learn about birthing babies, she seemed to be a natural.

His mind drifted and something about the way she stood, a hand on Mary Bonetrager's shoulder made a memory itch. He was a teenager and a troublemaker, according to his *daed* and the bishop. He'd been sitting on the front porch, and his *mamm* stood in front of him, her hand on his shoulder, and told him to straighten up. He was too smart to get snagged by the things of the world. He hadn't changed that day, but he'd slowly changed. The world still snagged him, but it was the call of higher education, not immorality, that seduced him away from the community.

He shook his head and forced himself to concentrate on his work.

Once his records were completed, he called the hospital to see how things were there. He'd rather be here, but his real job was priority.

"Memorial Hospital, this is Shannon, may I help you?"

"It's Daniel, is Dr. Jack with Lynda?" He'd found it was wise to get to know the names of as many of the staff as possible, even though it was difficult for him to talk to strangers with the easy familiarity that others, like Jack, seemed to manufacture as needed.

"Daniel, I hope you're not out in this weather." She didn't mince words with the news that made him stand and walk to a window. "Are you at home?"

Water fell down in sheets from the roof and splashed onto the dirt around them. "I'm at the Amish clinic. How did this happen so quickly?"

"It's more in your area than ours."

"I guess it's time to head back toward you." And get everyone else safely in their homes as soon as possible, he thought.

"I'd stay put. Roads are washing out, and there are flash floods. You're safer to stay where you are."

"Thank you, Shannon."

They hung up. The ground, already sodden from the spring rains, couldn't absorb another drop. Water gushed down the street.

"Daniel." Fannie stepped into his office. "The patients think they should leave. What do you think? Or should they stay and wait it out?" Fannie's concern was valid. Of course, if the patients stayed, it meant she and he would have to stay as well, though that wasn't really an issue for either of them, with no families waiting and concerned about them out in this. He chided himself. He might have no one, but Fannie still had Verna and Frieda. They would worry until she returned home.

"I suggest leaving. It's now or never." He stood by a window that was impossible to see through as gallons of water continued to fall.

"Dr. Kauffman, you have a phone. Did you hear when this will blow over?" A tall, thin Amish woman he didn't know peered over Fannie's shoulder into his office.

"Those at the hospital say it's not ending soon. I wish I had better information." And even more so, he wished he could be doing something with his idle hands. He walked to the waiting room and surveyed the few occupied chairs. "Did Mrs. Esch leave?"

"She decided to go to the market and wait there with her friend."

That left three women, plus Fannie and Lydia.

He gazed around the room and made a decision. He told the three women, "The bishop might not like it, but I'm driving you all home. This doesn't look like it's slowing any time soon."

The three women scrambled to their feet, talking excitedly about the prospect of a ride in Dr. Kauffman's truck.

He managed to fit them all in the cab of the truck and deposited them each at their doorsteps. The tall, skinny one lived nearby so in just a few minutes, they had more room.

As he wrestled the steering wheel to keep the truck

on the road, another car came into view. It drove slowly, which only made sense in this weather. But as the two cars neared, instead of the driver lifting a hand in greeting as was customary, the person behind the wheel—Daniel couldn't even say for sure if it was male or female—turned to scan the shops and homes along the other side of the street.

How odd.

The rain continued to pour in sheets, his windshield wipers unable to keep his view clear. He put the strange car out of his mind and concentrated on crawling along the rutted roads that quickly turned into mud lanes.

Finally an hour later he returned to the clinic. Lydia and Fannie were looking at a picture book, both heads bent over the tale of Peter Rabbit and Farmer MacGregor.

When they saw him, Fannie stood. "Well?" she asked, approaching him. "Is everyone safe?"

"They are. Now, I'll take Lydia to the Hershbergers." He extended his hand to the girl.

"Lydia should stay with me." Fannie also stretched a hand toward her.

He looked at both of them and dropped his hand. He'd leave it up to the two of them.

But it appeared Lydia had a say in where she might want to be. She hopped down from the chair and made her way toward them, except she moved past Fannie and slipped her hand into Daniel's.

For an instant Fannie looked hurt, then she shrugged.

"Are you all right?" He meant that Lydia wanted him instead of her.

She nodded and swallowed. "*Jah*. I just want her to feel safe, wherever that might be."

He believed that was true. There was some affection between the three of them that was beginning to grow.

"Now what?" she asked, but kept her eyes on Lydia.

"We'll wait until the rain stops." He moved closer to the window and watched as the drain spouts splashed gallons of water gushing down the gutter.

"I wonder how this will affect the crops and the planting. I've never seen this much water."

Lydia's silence could easily cause her to be forgotten at times. Fannie wondered if that was her way of staying away from people. Now, she moved in front of Fannie and looked out the window for herself.

"Keep positive, at least for the time being," Fannie murmured, more to herself than anyone else.

Daniel tapped her shoulder and motioned her to come a few steps back. She left Lydia watching the rain and followed Daniel to his office door.

"Do you think she can hear?" Daniel asked. He'd been thinking about having her tested but wasn't convinced he needed to go to such lengths.

Fannie stepped closer and kept her voice low. "She seems to be able to hear but it's selective. And seeing her responses to certain situations makes me wonder."

He frowned in surprise. "Perceptive of you to notice."

Fannie let out a sigh and looked around the room. Empty chairs lined the walls, magazines and children's books were scattered about. She tapped her foot.

"What are you thinking about?" Daniel asked.

"I guess we're staying?" She squeezed her hands together and glanced out the door.

Daniel noticed Lydia look at him when he was talking about the rain and other topics the adults were discussing. "Well, it's warm and dry in here. Unless you really want to be wet and cold, I think we should stay put and wait for this to pass." He winked at Fannie and smiled at Lydia, though both of them returned his gestures with worried expressions.

This little one knew more than she let on. It seemed she thought nothing was safe. He'd seen children beaten and abused, and she fit the profile.

As if she knew what he was thinking, she looked up at him and smiled.

If only they had some way of talking with her. Only time would tell if that would ever happen.

He felt the tremble begin in his fingers and work its way up his hand. He clutched his arm and pulled it close to his chest to hide the shaking from Fannie.

Lydia rapped on the glass.

Both he and Fannie turned to her. She pointed out the window.

Fannie strode over and looked. "It's stopped. The storm left as soon as it came. What do you make of that?" Fannie walked toward the door and picked up her bag.

Daniel followed more slowly. The trembling subsided until he felt he could let go of his arm in a natural manner. He dropped his hand to his side and looked out to the street.

"This isn't over," Daniel said. "The water still needs someplace to go."

Just like a certain blonde-haired, green-eyed young child. Actually just like him too. They all needed a place to go.

Chapter Twenty

"How does the garden look?" Frieda sat in the kitchen with one leg elevated.

"To be honest, it's not that bad. Your flowers took it the hardest." Fannie set the basket of onions, tomatoes, and peppers in the sink.

Verna stood at the counter, stirring pancake batter.

"I wish I could get in there and salvage what's left." Frieda watched their every move as she sat under the bright light of the kitchen table, obviously waiting for one of them to offer.

"Well, you can't, so just be happy we're willing to help you." Verna seemed to be more agitated lately, but Fannie didn't dare ask why. Either she continued to obsess about Fannie marrying or she was preoccupied with household tasks. "Fannie just picked everything that's ready."

"Fannie's a help." Frieda shifted on the chair. "But you don't seem to be concerned about the onions and tomatoes to make the picante sauce." Frieda's smug smile seemed to catch Verna off guard because her expression grew tight.

"Why did you get the notion to make such a

concoction?" Verna turned her back to them as she poured batter on the griddle, then sprinkled blueberries on each circle.

"So we don't have to eat your pancakes every morning." Frieda crossed her arms and waited.

Verna stopped dropping berries for a moment then added a few more. "I'll gladly prepare sour prunes for you instead of blueberry pancakes." She hummed quietly, with a smile of victory.

"Humph." Frieda's single word was heavy with portent. "You incorrigible woman." She tried to stand but sat back down when she couldn't seem to steady herself.

"You're a ridiculous old biddy." Verna flipped the first batch of pancakes.

Fannie would stay out of the ridiculous whirl of words but neither was listening to anyone but herself.

"I brought you into this *haus*..." Frieda flailed.

"I wish you hadn't."

Fannie sucked in air, unable to know what to say or to whom. Her head moved from one of them to the other, neither hearing what the other really said.

"*Stop!*" Fannie didn't recognize her own voice and took a step back. She cleared her throat and wrung her apron, not sure what to do next.

"Well, I know when I'm not wanted." Verna turned off the gas stove and went upstairs, each foot hitting the hardwood floor with venom.

Fannie watched her go then turned to *Mammi*. She wasn't sure who to console but decided to start where she was and hope this would blow over sooner than later. "Would you like me to help you make your picante sauce?"

Mammi's usual tough exterior seemed to melt a little, and Fannie saw a tear drop.

"Do you want to do it another day?" Fannie hoped she would hear a yes, but she knew Frieda's stubborn personality.

Mammi shook her head. "*Nee.* Don't want to waste good food. Best to get it done before it spoils."

"Okay then, no more complaining." Fannie knew better than to expect such a miracle, but she sincerely didn't want to live in a *haus* full of anger and resentment. "And pray for reconciliation so I'm not in the middle."

Frieda washed the tomatoes and handed Fannie the peppers to roast, obviously not wanting to talk, which suited Fannie just fine.

Fannie peeled the peppers and tried to think of something to say, but nothing seemed to be the right subject to bring up. The two women cooked together well, but having only two of the three of them in the kitchen seemed odd.

"The tomatoes look a little mushy." Fannie said out loud, then cringed. Perhaps but she shouldn't have said anything. She glanced at *Mammi* who didn't seem to have heard the judgment.

Footsteps tap-tapping from upstairs caught their attention.

Mamm descended the stairs and set her suitcase down at the bottom. She twined her fingers together. "I have all of my belongings and will be going into town to stay with Rose until I can arrange a carriage to go back home."

"*Mamm*—" Fannie stopped. She hated the thought of *Mamm* leaving angry, even though she would appreciate the peaceful home with her *mamm* only visiting and not living under the same roof.

Frieda scoffed.

Verna pointed at Frieda. "That is exactly why I have made this choice."

"If I ever did the eye rolling, this would be the time. I'm not going to stand here and listen to you both." Fannie sighed, unsure what to do without making matters worse. She wasn't an emotional person and this proved that fact. But she should be trying to sort things out regardless, helping both women to get along.

Verna walked through the kitchen with suitcase in hand. There would be less squabbling back and forth between the women. But then Fannie paused as the thought occurred to her: she was one of those squawking hens.

"I'm not sure what started this but stomping out is no way to solve anything." She sighed after looking at both of the women and thought of a way that might straighten things out.

"You want to go back South?" Thoughts of her *daed* passing away there crowded into her mind, and she didn't want to make any emotional decisions. But these were the realities her *mamm* would have to think about and face.

Verna glanced around the room as if this was the first time she'd ever seen it.

"You're being awfully rash about this, don't ya think?" Frieda placed a hand on her hip.

Verna stood tall. "I know when I'm not welcome."

"Humph."

Even Fannie was irritated with the same response.

"What is that noise? It's not even a real word." Verna stood tall and looked down her nose at Frieda.

Fannie decided to stand back and let them decide what to do. She went out on the front porch, but she could still hear their conversation. "You always..." and "You never..." seemed to be their theme, so she made her way to the flower garden. After a few minutes she realized she could still hear them and moved to the back of the house where the produce garden was. Spring onions, cabbage, lettuce, and peas all peeked through the sodden earth. The tomatoes had come from the greenhouse.

She enjoyed picking through some of the ripe vegetables and thought of all the delicious dishes she would make. But then she thought of how the three of them worked together to make meals.

Fannie stood and marched up the porch. She didn't want the harvest they grew together to end like this.

Verna whooshed by with her bag in tow.

"*Mamm*, let's make a rhubarb pie." She stood almost as tall as her mother and was almost as strong-willed.

"I will not." She walked down the creaky stairs, holding the banister. Frieda appeared in the doorway, leaning heavily on her cane.

This was worse than Fannie thought. The two women were known to disagree, but it usually simmered away as quickly as it boiled, unlike today.

For one of the few times in Fannie's life she was unsure what to do. Both women had their own points they felt were valid but neither would give in. The stomping, complaining, and unkind words lingered in the air still, like the aroma of bacon long after breakfast. But for a moment, all was quiet.

Fannie looked at Frieda who looked at Verna who promptly picked up her bag and started for the dirt road, leaving a trail of footsteps in the mud behind her.

"We can't let her go." Fannie kept her eye on Verna, hoping one of them would give in, but it didn't look that way.

"Stubborn as a mule," was all Frieda would say. She turned around to walk back into the *haus*.

So there Fannie stood with her *mamm* going one way and her *mammi* another. She wasn't one to get emotional, but she swallowed the sudden lump in her throat. It appeared neither was going to relent.

Chapter Twenty-One

Whack!

Daniel gave the thick trunk another hit. The old tree held a lot of memories. He and his brothers could actually hide behind it when they were skinny as rails. But being the oldest and overprotective, he never took advantage of the opportunity to climb it and hide in its limbs. He always worried someone would get hurt, which was why he was chopping the tree down. It was too close to the house if a harsh storm was to come their way. The Old Farmer's Almanac forecast a particularly wet spring. An old tree in sodden ground plus a high wind was a recipe for disaster.

He sat against the good size stump and draped his hand on his knee, just like he did as a kid.

"Want some company?" The female voice could only be from his mother, the person he missed more than anyone he had to leave behind.

"From you, always."

When she smiled, he did as well. Margaret Kauffman was a sturdy woman, but Daniel always thought of her as delicate. He thought it was perhaps because of the way she wilted under his *daed*'s cruelty.

"I've missed you. You were gone too long this time." She sat on the stump and ruffled his hair, just like she'd done when he was a boy. She swung her legs a bit, then crossed them at the ankle. Her black shoes gleamed in the sunlight.

He knew she meant what she said, and she was right. But other than the fall when he was not in demand so often, he didn't get to see her as much as he wanted to. Lately even when he was in the community, he was helping someone give birth or treating patients in the clinic.

"I come when I'm needed."

"I need you." She lifted her voice. "How long will you be here?"

"Long enough to chop up that big old tree." He stood and pointed at the branches looming over the house before he turned to face her look of sorrow.

"But I love that old tree." She looked up as the leaves moved in the wind.

"It's not safe anymore, *Mamm*."

She smiled at his change of language. "I like that…tree." His *mamm* smiled and closed her eyes against the brisk breeze.

He started to feel a little sentimental himself, then decided to keep it light. "Make for a lot of wood come winter."

"I'll ask Jonathan Burns next door to take some in return for finishing the chopping, splitting, and stacking." She turned to him. "I know you don't have that much time."

"I visited *Daed*." The words fell from his tongue before he could rein it in. He winced.

"And how is he?" Instead of hurt though, or anger, *Mamm* sounded placid and even interested.

"The same." Daniel kept his eyes on the honed edge of the ax.

"That's *gutt*."

"Is it?"

"It's better than him being worse, isn't it?"

"How can you be so calm?" he asked.

"I've had a lot of years of practice." She cocked her head at him. "And I've forgiven him, something that perhaps you have not yet done."

Frustration bubbled through him, and he hefted the ax for another swing.

"Daniel." *Mamm* spoke quietly, but it was enough for him to let the ax fall again.

"You are a healer of the body. No one is better at caring for his patients than you. But only *Gott* can heal the soul."

"*Mamm*—"

She raised a hand. "You had a hard time growing up. It's my fault for allowing your *daed* to stay when he was taking his anger and unhappiness out on all of us. I was afraid of what the community would say and do. But I know it was hard for you. Then you lost Emily. While you've been busy healing others, you've not allowed *Gott* to heal you."

His chest burned as her words sank into his spirit. He worked his jaw and swallowed hard. He nodded once.

"How long will you bless us with your presence this time?" she asked.

"Until the coming babies are all safe and sound." He forced his words to be light even as he wondered how long that would be.

"I didn't stop by just for the tree." He kept his eyes set forward.

"Oh." She studied his face. "What then?"

"Something out of the ordinary, at least for me. A wayward child came to the Lapp family."

She placed her hands on her cheeks. "They didn't take in a relative's child. I would have known."

"Well, a lost girl ended up at their home and they might need some help."

"*Ach*, poor child. Why the Lapps?"

Her lack of urgency surprised him.

"They found her in their barn, no other reason."

"She needs a loving family." *Mamm* turned to him, waiting.

"I agree. Which is why she's with the Lapps."

Mamm's silence was deafening.

"Are you saying I should get in the middle of this?"

"You already have."

Those were the words he didn't want to hear. His life was at the hospital. This prolonged season in the community was a one-time thing.

"The commitment you made for deliveries should be honored or you should hand over the responsibility." Her eyes never wavered. "And who would you suggest to take my place?" He was a bit irritated by her assumption that he shouldn't deliver babies in the community. Was she seeing something he was missing? "And I enjoy both, the hospital work and the babies here." Then he stopped and glanced at the waning light; the flower petals glowed as if illuminated from the inside. The pinks and oranges and yellows seemed lit by God's grace.

It felt as if God was right there with him, which was a confusing thought considering he hadn't given his faith much attention since he started practicing medicine. The discomfort made him stop thinking those thoughts and put down the ax.

"What is it, son?" *Mamm* pushed off the grass underneath her.

He helped her off the stump and felt the need to leave. "I should go."

"No more tree cutting?" She tilted her head, studying him.

"I have some things to do." He hadn't made much progress with the tree anyway. It could wait. "I'll try to finish it up before you return from Ohio, but I can't make any promises."

He walked with her to his truck, hoping she wouldn't ask any more questions.

She stopped, put her hands on his cheeks, tilted his head down, and kissed the top of his head. "You're a special man, Daniel."

The sense he had just a few minutes ago of God being with him was not something to be casually dismissed.

He stuck his hands in his pockets and watched her walk back to the only real home he'd ever known.

Chapter Twenty-Two

"Where could he be?" Fannie said under her breath. She didn't want to attract too much attention from the *mamm* and so betray her own nerves.

The mother-to-be was wailing like Fannie had never heard. At first she thought the woman must surely need to go to the hospital; only someone in horrible pain and distress would act in such a way.

Slam! The front door vibrated with tension as someone hurled it closed.

Fannie hoped and prayed it was Daniel. The families and neighbors were wearing out the wood floor while they waited.

Sure enough, Daniel strode into the room a few seconds later and Fannie let out a brief sigh. "What kept you?" She knew better than to ask but curiosity got the best of her. She was just irritated enough to demand some answers.

Daniel didn't respond but simply shifted to one side then washed his hands. "I got here as fast as I could."

Fannie glanced at him, unsure how much further to press the issue.

She moved from the dresser, covered with cloths and lukewarm water, to his side.

Daniel nodded to Fannie, not waiting a moment. "Towel."

Fannie let out a breath and picked up the piece of linen, then handed it to Daniel. Their communication was stressed, a rapid pace.

This knowledge concerned her. "Do we need outside help? The hospital?" she murmured into his ear as he dried his hands.

Daniel looked at something behind her.

Fannie turned and saw Cindy walk into the room.

It all made sense now. They'd known this might be a difficult delivery and Daniel wanted a "real" nurse here for this one.

Fannie was too surprised to know either how she felt or her role to play at this point.

"Cindy, forceps. Fannie, water bath."

"No C-section?" Cindy hadn't acknowledged Fannie since she came into the room, but this was a sensitive delivery, so Fannie would leave it at that.

Besides, the cesarean was one procedure Fannie couldn't imagine them using, but at this point she would hope for the best.

"No, last resort." He didn't even look at the mother; there was no time to explain. Something was wrong.

Cindy and Daniel worked together, side-by-side, preparing for whatever possible scenario was ahead.

It wasn't long before the babe made its entrance into the world, *mamm* howling, and *daed* pacing outside the room.

When the *daed* heard the newborn crying, he burst through the door.

Fannie frowned at him, wishing he'd waited for someone to call him into the room. She still wasn't sure whether *mamm* and babe were okay. She bent over the *mamm* and out of the corner of her eye she watched Daniel and Cindy confer over the baby.

Perhaps, in this case, it was best for the *daed* to be with the *mamm*.

"Anything I should do?" The *daed* wiped his palms on his pants, waiting for what he probably hoped would be a no.

Fannie was about to answer and give him a task to keep him occupied, but Cindy looked up and said the opposite. "No, you just make yourself comfortable."

Fannie scoffed inwardly. What new father would be comfortable at this moment? Or was she being petty?

Fannie helped the mother sit up in her bed. Cindy placed the swaddled infant in the *mamm*'s arms.

"What is wrong with this little one?" Fannie whispered to Daniel. She hated humbling herself to ask, but her curiosity was greater than her fear of appearing ignorant.

"The syndrome that many Amish pass to their babies when they intermarry. I'll recommend they see Dr. Holmes at the Clinic for Special Children."

Fannie had wondered if that might be an issue but didn't want to speculate. She remembered her own niece, born so small and yet doing better than ever expected thanks to the clinic. If there was to be a good outcome, Dr. Holmes was the babe's best option.

As families began to come and enjoy God's gift of

another child, Fannie chatted among them as Daniel and Cindy cleaned up, and he put his notes together.

When they finished, Fannie thought it only right to say good-bye to the pair. If only she was in the right mood she would commend them on their efficiency. Although it was hard for her, she needed to accept the idea of Cindy and Daniel working together without her. The sooner, the better, in fact.

Chapter Twenty-Three

"Don't forget Amish healing." Doc Rueben surveyed Daniel as Doc's wife handed him a handful of hazelnuts.

Daniel stood watching with arms crossed. "Do you really think this is going to help her memory?"

The old doc seemed determined to show Daniel that his way of doing medicine was better than the modern way. "*Jah*, that's it."

"So now what?" Daniel leaned against the wall with arms folded. He almost shook his head as Doc brought out green peppers, cloves, dates, ginger root, and muskmelon seeds and mixed in olive oil and hazelnuts in equal quantities.

"Anything else?" Daniel stepped closer to examine the concoction. "There sure are a lot of different herbs in there."

"Actually yes, but I didn't want to bore you by listing them all."

Daniel let out a breath, knowing he was being too skeptical. He had seen Amish doctors treat their patients with great success so he should give Doc Reuben a chance to prove himself. But it was hard, knowing, at least in his opinion, there was something more reliable available.

"I agree that these can help, but perhaps not to the capacity needed in some situations."

Doc stopped. "I suppose we will have to agree to disagree."

"Maybe we should table this until a different day." Daniel hoped that was enough for the time being.

"Where are you off to in such a hurry?" Doc seemed almost disappointed, but Daniel had no time for that now.

"Sorry, Doc. Duty calls. Please tell your wife thanks for lunch. It was wonderful."

"I'll do that, and next time I'd like to have little Lydia come by. She doesn't say much, but she's the sweetest little one around."

Daniel knew full well he said that about all the children, but there was no sense in reminding him of that. Daniel agreed. Lydia was different.

"I'll be sure and do that." He paused and turned around. "Did you say Lydia doesn't speak much?"

"*Jah*, why?" He squinted his eyes at Daniel.

"You've heard her talk?"

"*Nee*." He lifted his chin. "But I wonder if she can't talk or if she chooses not to." He shrugged. "But she is who she is."

As Daniel left Doc's, he thought about how much he greatly appreciated the way the community had taken the child in. He'd felt a connection between the two of them, so he felt responsible for her, but then everyone had accepted her as their own.

And then there was the car that he'd seen driving

slowly through the community during the rainstorm. It was probably a tourist bold enough to come into the community. But it may have been the child's family looking for her. He resolved to keep an eye open and be alert for any more strangers.

As he drove through the community he noticed a group gathering on the bishop's back lawn and setting down three empty bags.

Daniel smiled. Nothing like a game of baseball with the Amish, one of the many things he missed. He pulled to the side of the road and glanced around to see if Fannie was around. If nothing else he could tell her about Doc's regard for Lydia.

"Well, look's who's here."

Daniel said a silent prayer and turned toward the voice.

"Afternoon." The bishop's voice thundered in his head.

"And to you."

"What brings you here?"

Daniel didn't miss a beat. "Birthing your next generation."

The crusty old man made him want to say more than he should. Instead he stuck his hands in his pockets, an act forbidden to the Amish, and waited for the bishop to scold him. All Daniel had to do from there was let him make a fool of himself. Every pregnant Amish woman would be up in arms if the bishop denied Daniel the access needed to deliver their babies.

The bishop pulled back and stuck out his bottom lip. "I see. Although you have not spoken to me about this."

Daniel held back the words he was thinking and let out a breath. "There has never been any issue before."

"Maybe so, maybe not." He frowned.

The bishop had often been difficult to deal with in the past, but now he seemed even more obstinate.

"How long do you expect to be here?" The bishop tilted his head to one side and waited for an answer.

Daniel looked down the sun-lit valley with flowing green leaves blowing away against the sun. This was what he missed. The quiet. The stillness around him waiting for the sun to dip down behind the horizon.

But this could never be for him. He had worked too hard and too long to go backward. The thought of giving up so much to gain so little was ridiculous. He shrugged. "As long as I'm needed for the deliveries this spring. Then I'll be back to the hospital full time."

The bishop grunted. "*Gutt.* Now, I've heard something about a young girl who has come to our community. Is this so?"

Daniel knew word would get around about Lydia, but he'd hoped for more time before the bishop got himself involved. There was something about the girl that made him think he should protect her.

"Lydia." Daniel would give the man as little information as possible. Though in actuality, he didn't have enough information to make a difference anyway.

Chapter Twenty-Four

The wind was picking up so Fannie paused in front of the bakery where she'd been working all morning. She held down her dress with one hand and kept her *kapp* in place with the other.

She headed for home. As she passed the bishop's *haus*, though, she saw Daniel in conversation with him. She thought perhaps they were talking about Lydia. The bishop was the only one who had a problem with the child, which was expected. The man seemed to dislike everyone and everything, though she wasn't sure why.

She wondered if Daniel needed some help explaining how the child came to the community. *Nee*, not likely. Still, it would be nice to see Daniel and talk for a moment. She needed to ask him something anyway.

After stopping the buggy and tying down her horse, who was growing more worn and tired by the day, she eyed the two men deep in conversation.

As she approached, she heard them indeed talking about Lydia. Fannie increased her pace.

"Why are you coming to me with this?" Daniel asked.

"There must be others who care about her as well." His response wasn't a surprise.

"But someone brought her into our midst. I figured it might be you. And others agreed. So what do you have to say?"

"As long as Social Services gave the Lapps temporary custody, she's in good hands."

Fannie heard that note of finality in Daniel's voice when he was done with a subject.

She sighed. This would not go well. It seemed the bishop hadn't forgiven Daniel for leaving, and she'd heard that he swore he would never let him come back to the community. Even the service Daniel provided for the expectant mothers seemed to anger him.

Fannie was now close enough to see Daniel's profile. His jaw twitched, and his stature was straight as an arrow.

"*Hallo*, Fannie." The bishop stopped what he was saying and gave her a second look and then turned back to Daniel.

Fannie stopped at Daniel's side and crossed her arms. She hoped that was enough to still their conversation, at least for now.

"We'll talk about this at a better time." The bishop nodded to her and retreated slowly, as if he didn't feel comfortable turning his back on them.

When he was far enough away, she started asking questions. "What was that about? Is he angry about Lydia? Is he going to send her away?"

Daniel just shook his head.

The tension between Daniel and the bishop grated on her, and she felt she should go to him with her thoughts.

He seemed to be getting worse in his old age, and she had lost her patience. First, he had refused to allow Daniel to leave for medical school, and he still seemed to have a grudge against him. Now he'd taken an unreasonable attitude about Lydia, probably because Daniel was the one who found her.

Fannie watched as the bishop walked toward those gathered for the game, limping slightly. Fannie noticed he didn't mingle or chat with anyone. He just kept his slow pace until he found a chair. Maybe she was too hard on the man, but he made it hard for her to show much sympathy.

"You're staring." Daniel's voice brought her back.

"*Jah*, I guess I am." She looked over at him in wonder that he seemed to be getting more handsome each day. "I need to let go of some of my anger."

"It's good to know talking with the bishop makes you feel so vulnerable." He grinned and started walking. "But he is the bishop and is only doing what he thinks is right."

"*Jah*, I wouldn't want to be in his shoes." She walked by his side. "Actually I could see you as a deacon or minister of some sort, one who plays those roles. If you weren't shunned."

Daniel sighed. "There lies the problem. I'm not under the *Meidung*, but many people feel I should be."

She furrowed her brow and let the comment go. As much as she would like to work with him even more in her own community, it could never happen due to his leaving so long ago.

Small drops of rain began, first lightly then they slowly built up. "We're in for more rain. And the ground is still sodden from the last storm. This could be bad."

He pointed to the dark clouds moving across the sky, and she sucked in a breath.

"I need to get home." She picked up her skirts and dashed back to the road.

Huge pockets of slow swirling charcoal-colored clouds grew against the sky. A shiver went down her back as the mass continued to grow.

Daniel followed her. "Let me drive you in the truck." He grabbed her hand and tried to tug her to a stop.

But she pulled away. "I'll make better time if I cut through Beaver Dam Field on foot. I'll be home before you can drive on the roads. The bishop will let me keep my horse and buggy in his barn."

His jaw tightened as he followed her to secure her horse and buggy, but he didn't argue.

"I've never seen anything like this before." The rain was setting in so fast. She stared at the angry clouds until hard drops of water hit her cheek, arm, and then most any part of her body. "I have to go. I don't want to get stuck here at the bishop's *haus*."

"I'm not leaving you alone out in this."

She felt his hand again, but this time he ran alongside her, pulling her with him as he ran, faster than she could keep up with. But she couldn't—shouldn't—stop him from running from what sounded like a roaring lion behind them.

They ran between houses and started across the field that bordered the lane leading to her *Mammi*'s *haus*.

Too scared to look back, she let him yank her one way and then another to avoid holes and shrubs. A mass of dirty branches and other debris tumbled around them. Leaves, dirt, tree limbs, and litter blew across their path.

With no way to see what lie before her, she kept her eyes on the ground so as not to trip and fall. Rain fell, but the ground was still sodden from the last storm and the water had nowhere to go. Drops gathered into puddles and ran in streams from one low spot in the field to another, then down the embankment and into the river. Grasses bent under the force of the wind and rain.

A sting on her cheek made her wince, and she lifted a hand against it. What was so powerful that it could be dragging them into this, what seemed to be a never-ending field of mud?

A hill rose in front of them. They attacked it at a run, but the grass, slick from the rain, conspired to send them back to the bottom. Their feet found no traction on the slippery slope.

"Keep up!" Daniel didn't turn back to see her, just kept pulling her up, over, and through whatever part of the terrain wouldn't toss them down to the bottom.

Fannie wanted to look back at the river to see how far the water was rising, how far they were from the swiftly flowing river.

He yanked her arm. "Keep your eyes on me." He yelled through the gnashing of earth and wind.

The strength of his shout brought more anxiety, but it also brought up the strength necessary to continue climbing the hill.

The ground under them began to shudder.

"The hill is going to slide down to the river." Daniel grabbed her hand and pulled her the last few feet to the top of the ridge.

The ground tumbled away from her. Mud and roots and grass churned toward the river.

"We have to stay ahead of it." Daniel's grunts became a painful yell. Surely his arm ached from having pulled her up most of the way. She glanced over at him to see his face contorted and the veins on his arm bulging.

The earth stilled and he turned. "We should be far enough from the river now."

She stood tall and caught up to him, and then stayed by his side. Fannie slipped and nearly went down on her bottom. Walking was getting harder with each step or slip.

Daniel lowered his head and put his hands on his knees. "You okay?"

She nodded. The wind was too loud for him to hear her voice. But it was a lie. She'd never been so scared.

Daniel put out his hand, but she refused. She could tell he was spent after getting her so far. He shook his head and motioned for her to continue before him, but she didn't leave his side.

She glanced behind her to see lightning arc in the sky. The trees crashing into each other in the wind was bad enough, but with the water still building up around them, there was no place for shelter.

"Stay with me," Daniel told her.

She had every intention of doing just that, but hearing his voice made her feel a bit better. He was scared too.

"Where is there to go?" she asked. The ground still shivered under their feet. How could they be certain which direction held safety and which held danger?

"I don't know, but we can't stay put." He yelled but she could barely hear him. The powerful rain had them trapped on every side.

Fannie started to panic. She needed to do something, but what?

Rocks began to move in the mud, pushed by the overwhelming streams that formed in every direction. All the water rushed to reunite in the river, but it carried along mud and bushes and rocks in its haste.

Daniel walked over to her and crouched down. "This isn't going to be easy, and it's not going away. But we have to use our heads and figure out a way to get out of this relentless storm." He wiped his face with one hand, and it was immediately covered with water again. And the rain was falling even harder.

"What are our options?" She didn't believe he had any ideas, but she could hope.

"We can't fight the mudslide, but we have to find a way down. There's no going up." He nodded up to where they were supposed to be going. "The worst would be the trees uprooting, like some did as we were climbing."

"*Jah.* But not many seem small enough to fall." She couldn't say she truly believed that, but she was hoping it was true.

"I hope you're right but don't count on it. Let's try there." He nodded to where the debris was least intimidating.

She followed, seeing nowhere else to go.

Chapter Twenty-Five

When the light started to fade, Daniel began to worry. He thought they would find a *haus* or at least be closer to where they should be going by this time.

"We're lost, aren't we?" Fannie looked at him with soulful eyes and watched him intently until he answered.

He pursed his lips. "I hope not or this will be a long night." And a cold one, but he didn't want to remind her of that.

She held herself tightly and began to shiver. It wasn't as cold as it had been, but it would be soon.

"Tell me what you're really thinking." He kept his eyes on her, and she began to tremble again.

Fannie looked around the area and then at him. "I'm scared...and worried because it's going to be dark soon. And I'm cold and hungry."

Her honesty told Daniel to start thinking about home. He didn't know her to be a worrier; she was a fixer. This didn't fit her.

She shook her head, seeming to free herself of the fear of the last few minutes. "Sorry, I—"

"There's nothing to be sorry about. We're in a difficult situation, and we're concerned. As we should be."

She frowned. "That's not very encouraging." Her brows drew together.

"I don't mean to be negative, I just want us to be prepared for whatever might come our way." He turned to her and rubbed her arms to warm her up.

When he looked at her, he felt responsible. He didn't know why specifically, maybe just because he was a doctor or the man who should know what to do and say. But at this moment he felt much like her. Uncertain. A bit worried. Scared, even.

With the sun going down, he scrambled to take action. They might not have much, but they could at least be doing something to keep warm until help came along. But in all reality everyone below was probably keeping account of their own families, not a visiting doctor and a near-spinster midwife.

He instantly chided himself. He of all people knew Fannie was much more than that. Her *mammi* would be concerned when Fannie didn't return.

"Maybe we should back track so they can find us more easily." She rubbed her arms again and he felt the guilt with it. He should be thinking of something.

"Let's think of positives. Our clothes are heavy and warm, and that's huge. Right?"

"*Jah*. And wet." She didn't seem impressed but he was desperate for her to stop worrying. He wanted to diagnose the situation and solve it. Perhaps it was partly his medical training, but there also was just something about Fannie that made him yearn to please her.

"And the sun is still up."

She looked over her shoulder to see the edge of the sun slowly sinking into the horizon. She frowned. "Not for long."

"The rain has stopped. If we keep moving, our clothes will dry out. So it looks like we should keep walking or try to find someplace to wait out the night." Daniel wasn't sure what was protocol in this situation, but it didn't matter.

He looked around at the sodden landscape. The rain had stopped, but the trees continued to drip. Maybe they were closer than they thought. It felt like they'd run for miles, but through the rain and wind and debris, it couldn't have been that far. He cast a rational eye, calculating how long they had been running and the direction in which they ran. They could be right above the schoolhouse. Of course, the mudslide meant the ground was unstable and it wasn't safe to descend. They would have to move east or west along the ridge to find their way back.

He came to a decision. "Let's keep moving."

Fannie sighed.

She didn't have much more in her, he could tell, but he wanted to give it one more try before they ended up in darkness.

"Can you do that for me? Walk a ways?" He wouldn't take no for an answer, so he hoped she would cooperate.

All he got was a nod and her starting to walk again. This time he walked behind her. He would have to maneuver her somewhat, but at least this way he knew she was keeping up.

They both stopped after a few yards, trying to see

what was in the air. "Smells like smoke," Daniel finally said.

"*Jah*, that means we're close to someone, right?" She looked up, down, and around after keeping her eyes downward so as not to trip or fall. The fatigue was getting the best of her. He read it in the droop of her shoulders, her heaving chest, the dullness in her eyes. They would have to stop for the night.

"I think it's farther than it seems." He was about to explain his thoughts when she turned around and stared at him. Her face was taut, and her chest moved quickly.

"I'm too cold to stay here and too tired to walk. There's no good answer." The concern in her eyes was enough for him to leave the decision up to her.

"So pick one or the other." He would have to hold his tongue. Once the sun went down they wouldn't get enough warmth to sleep; it would be a miserable night of constant cold. "Do we walk or do we rest?"

"I need a break. At least a short one." She looked around and found a makeshift seat on a rock.

He was about to encourage her to keep going, because if they didn't it would just be harder to get going again. But then he saw her bow her head and begin to pray.

He took the two steps between them and wrapped his arms around her. She seemed too tired to cry.

He laid his head to the side. "I saw a rock formation not too far back, if you want to stay there for the night."

She nodded. "Thank you. I know it's selfish of me, but I just need a minute to rest. That's all. I hope *Mamm* and *Mammi* are okay."

He pulled her up and slipped an arm under hers so he could half-carry her to the rocks. "I know. I shouldn't have been so hard on you." She was surely exhausted and hungry. This was the least he could do for her. "Your *Mamm* is farther south in town at your Great-Aunt Rose's, and Frieda should be fine. She always is, and she's in a solid and warm home without many trees close by."

Going backward was killing him. But he had to be patient. He hoped this rest would be enough to get her rejuvenated.

A rock to sit on with an entrance to a small cave opening was hardly a place to rest, but he'd make the best of it.

"We could be getting closer, but instead I pull us back." A tear slipped down one cheek, and she quickly wiped it away.

He shook his head. "This is no one's fault; it just is."

She lifted her head and lifted one side of her mouth. "You're a kind man when you want to be."

He chuckled. "That was a compliment. I think." He smiled. "Can I ask you a question?"

Fannie's brow furrowed. "You are not one to ever ask permission to ask a personal question, so I'm not sure how to respond. But I am too interested to say no. What is your question?"

"Why haven't you ever been betrothed?"

She sat up tall and took a beat before answering. "I don't know the answer to that question."

He realized his mistake and groped for something to say. "I hope the rest does you good. Enough to get home."

"It will. Tonight or tomorrow. God knows."

"You know what I'd like about now? A piece of your shoo-fly pie."

She turned her head toward him. "I didn't think you liked my pie since you didn't eat a second slice."

She was responding with her usual starchiness, which he took as a good sign.

"You were probably giving me a hard time so I didn't tell you that I liked it at the time." He cocked his head to one side. "Maybe I should try it again."

He stared at her lips too long before remembering that they were alone.

Chapter Twenty-Six

Jannie watched Daniel retreat before her eyes. One minute he was open and welcoming, and the next he was cold as ice. It was difficult to keep up with him. Not that she wanted to. She should stay out of it. But against her better judgment, there was something about him that interested her.

"You asked me a question. May I ask you one?"

His brown eyes were unfathomable, but he inclined his head slightly.

"You said you went overseas?" She'd always wanted to ask but didn't want to look interested.

He nodded, still not revealing much about what he was thinking.

"What was it like?"

"I've visited Zimbabwe a couple of times. I'd always wanted to go to Africa to help the people there."

"Did you...like it, I mean?"

"I never felt more alive. I had a purpose in life. But then things took a turn the last time I went when my father left my mother while I was gone."

"Can I ask what happened?" She had become so

interested in him she couldn't help but ask. Leaving a spouse in the Amish order was rare, so it must be difficult for him to talk about.

He paused and then looked over at her, as if not wanting to tell her but then he spoke. "My father wasn't good to my mother. She finally asked him to leave, and he did. Without question."

"How did your mother make it?"

"Surprisingly she has done well enough on her own." He looked over at Fannie for the first time since talking about his parents. "Between the garden and her chickens, she makes enough to buy the things she can't produce on her own."

"I'm sorry about your parents, Daniel. I do remember hearing something about it, but I've never spent much time with Margaret." Fannie hoped she hadn't overstepped her boundaries. But it helped her understand him better.

He chewed the inside of his mouth and then glanced at her, maybe having second thoughts about confiding in her? His left hand trembled a bit as he stuck it in his pants pocket. Surely he was as exhausted as she and welcomed this respite.

"You know I will keep this between us, don't you?"

He smiled and nodded. "I appreciate that and expect nothing less from you." He shrugged, and his grin grew a little. "Well, there is something else I'd like to expect."

"What to do you mean?" As soon as she asked, she wondered if she was getting herself into something that wasn't her business. Of course it wasn't. She was just fooling herself, thinking she wanted to take care of him and his shattered family.

He just shook his head and rubbed his elbow.

"Have you seen your *daed* since the last time you stopped by his *haus*?" There she went again, but she was full of so many questions.

He turned to her. "No, but even that seems like a lifetime ago."

She nervously persisted, hoping she wasn't pushing too far. "Do you think you'll visit him again?"

Daniel let out a slow breath. "I've learned my lesson. I'll check up on him from time to time, but I won't push him to be a real father in my life. He's just too bitter."

"Bitter?" What Fannie saw in his eyes wasn't hurt as much as disappointment.

Daniel half smiled. "He expected my mother to be shunned for asking him to leave, but the community knew he was difficult, and they stood by her. He's angry that no one sees things his way."

He rubbed a hand across his forehead. "My mom says I need to forgive him. That's what she's done, and she seems to be at peace with everything. At least, more at peace than I've been. But it's hard to forget the pain he put us all through."

"Forgiving and forgetting aren't the same thing. I think your *mamm* is right."

She cleared her throat and looked away, wanting to change the subject.

"I wonder what Lydia is doing right now."

He smiled. "You've become fond of her."

She hoped he felt the same about the young one. He seemed to when they first found her. "*Jah*, but she seems to be comfortable with the Lapps, with all their girls."

"I'm sure you're right. I still want to get to the bottom

of it though. It's too strange to just let it go, to never know where she came from."

"Or where her family is."

"I have a feeling they might be the reason she's here."

"What do you mean, that they didn't take care of her?" It was a horrible thought. Not in their community. No one would mistreat or neglect a child.

"If she were a little older, I might think she had run away from home and wasn't lost at all. That's not uncommon for abused or neglected children to do, but it doesn't usually work out well."

She knew he was right to be concerned about what brought Lydia to them, but she didn't want to add that to her concerns at the moment. They had to figure out how to get back home.

The silence lengthened, and she leaned against the rock, letting the ache in her shoulders ease. She drifted into a light sleep.

"Fannie."

She blinked. Daniel in her home, waking her from a nap? *Nee*, it couldn't be. She lifted her head, and the pain in her arms and legs recalled her to reality. They were in a cave, in the hills outside town. A horrible storm. The mudslide.

"Are you ready to walk again?" By the way he asked she didn't think there was any option, but he was right. They needed to try to get back to town and to safety—if there was a town left after the wall of mud that fell out from under their feet yesterday.

"*Jah*, I'm not looking forward to the elements, but it's not much better here. How far do you think we are from the *haus*?" She stood and they emerged from the shelter of the rocks.

"Not as far as we think. The storm made it seem farther than it really was, in my opinion anyway."

Fannie stared through the lightly spitting rain. It could be worse so she counted her blessings and hoped for the sun to shine soon.

"Let's get this done." He passed by her, which made her pick up the pace. He kept his eyes sharp, and she realized he was tracking backward to the way they came.

After what seemed longer than she hoped, she had to ask. "How much farther do we have to go?"

"If my calculations are correct we're making good time, so we might be even closer than I originally thought."

She held in a breath and let it out, not wanting to be disappointed if he was wrong. But Daniel seemed to have a good sense of direction. The terrain was worse the closer they got to the community. Rocks and mud filled their way. They had to maneuver around uprooted trees, their roots pointing skyward like an old *mammi*'s arthritic fingers.

Daniel looked from side to side. The closer they got to the river, the worse the damage was. This landslide had taken its toll.

Daniel stopped, and Fannie looked over to see where he was looking. Their little community had become what Fannie could only describe as a mud hole. A few people walked through the mess and debris, but most seemed to be nestled in their homes. They were probably doing what they could to salvage their crops, which were most likely washed away.

"Oh, my," was all she could think to say. She felt helpless against all the damage.

They scrambled down the rest of the hill and hurried through the field. As they entered the outskirts of the community, they came to a stop, surveying the damage. Fences were gone, mud filled kitchen gardens, and dogs wandered about with their coats clinging to their shivering bodies.

"No." Daniel whispered. Fannie followed where he was looking to see a small body wrapped with a sheet on a front porch.

The first thing she thought of was Lydia. She dashed to the porch, fell to her knees, and pulled the sheet away with shaking fingers. She released a pent-up sigh and sagged back on her hands. A bundle of blankets and quilts, not a child. The sheet, she supposed, was meant to keep off the worst of the dirt. She covered up the stack again and moved it closer to the door, away from the still-dripping *haus* eaves.

"Let's go." Daniel started to walk between the *hauses*, and she stayed by his side.

When they finally got to the school, all was a bustle. Some had buckets and were scooping up the water still running down the streets. They threw the water down a makeshift waterfall away from the community and toward the river.

"There is a lot to do here." He looked from side to side assessing the area. With his knowledge she felt confident he could help make this right.

"How bad is it?" She had a hard time looking around, worried she might see something she didn't want to. But she would go to her family first and foremost.

"Could be worse, but we haven't covered the whole area yet." He looked over at her quickly. "Go to your family. You'll be ready to work once you know they're okay."

"*Jah*. And you'll check on your *mamm*?"

He shook his head. "She's visiting family in Ohio." But he worried about the old tree he still hadn't gotten around to cutting.

"Thank *Gott*."

He nodded. "Thank God, indeed. I couldn't do anything if I thought she was in danger."

"How did all this happen and so quickly?" She was still eager to get to her family's farm but also reluctant to leave him.

"There have been too many storms for us not to have a landslide sooner or later. The farmers use the good soil on the higher ground. It washes away easily, leaving the homes in the lower areas vulnerable to something like this."

"Why haven't we done something about it?"

"If I was asked, I'd do my part." He turned to her again. "In case you haven't noticed, I'm not welcomed by all who live here."

"Well, that might change if you solve this problem." She lifted a brow and gave him a look.

"It's not that easy, and you know it." He was changing his thoughts; she knew by his expressions.

"Just do what you do best." She squeezed his arm. "Since when did anything stop you from doing what you were made to do?"

He stopped and slowly turned his eyes toward her. "I've never heard it said like that."

“Well, now you have.” She tilted her head for extra measure.

He grinned. “You’re pretty amazing.” And with that he started walking, looking from side to side, likely assessing the needed repairs and who needed medical attention or food and shelter.

Chapter Twenty-Seven

In the days after the landslide the uprooted trees and mud were constant reminders of their situation, as were the leaking roofs and flooding still in many of their homes. Most families refused to leave their homes, which irritated Daniel. Until the homes were safe to live in, no one should stay. Still, some were fortunate enough to have not sustained much damage and weren't in need of any help.

"Stubborn Amish..." Daniel sat on a stool in the clinic, calculating how many needed assistance and how much he was needed in the community versus the hospital, which was his paying job.

He leaned back in the rickety building that was used only for his work here—checkups, medicine, shots, and so on.

"I brought you some tea." Fannie's voice was what he needed, and the tea was fine, although he preferred coffee.

"Anything warm to drink is good for now. Thanks." He accepted the cup from her.

"You're welcome." She half smiled at him and he

smiled in return. She was always doing something, never a moment to spare.

"What's on the agenda?" he asked as he looked over some notes.

"Word is that if the area doesn't meet the living conditions inspection we might be evacuated."

He stopped what he was reading and stared at her. "I can't imagine people being sent away." He turned to her.

"I suppose we could be." She paused again and frowned. "Many of the houses and barns are pretty weak from all the rocks and debris that slammed into them."

"A lot of the trees are also unstable, and some are broken. I hadn't thought about it, but the county authorities have the right to check just about everything, and people might have to share their homes."

"What about you? Will you stay?" She stared and waited.

"I'll...go where I'm needed most."

"That's good of you. But you might be needed to help in other places. Like the hospital?"

He shrugged. "It's possible."

She stood. "Let's see what's going on outside." She waved for him to follow her.

Outside a parade of people busily brought their belongings in carts or searched for a place for their possessions, or at least that's what it seemed to him.

Daniel felt a tug on his pants and looked down to see Lydia gazing up at him. He smiled, and she moved closer and allowed him to pick her up. Having been so timid before, there had been a definite change.

"How are you, little one?"

She pulled her jacket around her and shivered.

"You're cold."

She didn't reply.

He pointed to his shirt. "Let's put this on you."

He put her down, then took it slow, moving carefully to take off his outer layer. He still had a thermal shirt on. He handed her the plaid flannel.

"Put your hands up." She did, which showed him her hearing was good. That made him wonder all the more if she could speak too.

He glanced at Fannie, who had her hand over her mouth, obviously touched by the bond growing between them.

"You've been a brave girl."

She looked up at him for just a second and then looked away. It was difficult to know what she was thinking and what she could and couldn't do. When things settled down, he would like to have a good amount of time with her to find out more.

They approached the schoolhouse and went inside.

"She was with the Lapps during the storm, in case you were wondering." Fannie watched Lydia scan the room then scamper off to join Miriam.

"Couldn't ask for a better family for her," he said.

The way Fannie gazed at him made his heart skip a beat. He swallowed to be sure he could speak normally. "Even though there haven't been any leads from the police department, that doesn't mean she is here to stay."

"The social worker has no problem with her staying with the Lapps. She doesn't need any more disruptions in her life." Fannie spoke firmly, as if she knew what was best for the child.

"At least not now. But there will be a day." He wanted

to caution Fannie, to tell her not to get too attached to Lydia, or whatever her name was. Someone could turn up and claim her, and Fannie would have to watch her leave. He smiled to blunt the harsh truth. "But we'll hope and pray it's not for a while."

He surveyed the room, then paused as his eyes lit on James Miller, who was making his way toward them, his gaze firmly fixed on Fannie.

"Fannie, I've been looking for you. Are you okay?" James didn't even acknowledge Daniel.

"*Jah*, I'm fine." Her tone was puzzling.

"Thank *Gott*." He reached for her hand. "Daniel, would you excuse us? I need to have a private conversation with Fannie."

Daniel turned and made his way outside again and instructed himself to ignore the gnawing ache in his heart. Daniel had no claim on her. He couldn't offer her a life away from her home and family. And he had no future here. The bishop made it very clear he couldn't come back. Even if the bishop changed his mind, Daniel still had hefty student loans to pay off before he could think about a different sort of future.

He needed to go to the hospital. The days missed were understandable, but he knew he needed to go back. He would surely see some of the Amish there as well. It would take long hours and much work to repair all that was lost. There were no deaths, which was most important. But that didn't mean some wouldn't be going to the hospital when Doc Rueben couldn't give them what they needed.

His tremor was worse, coming more frequently. That seemed understandable considering everything he'd done in the last few days. He'd think about it later. There was too much going on at the moment.

Fannie appeared at his side, her hands wrapped in her apron, pulling and twisting the fabric.

"Everything okay?" he asked. A wave of protectiveness surged in his chest. "Did James . . . ?" His voice trailed off. Whatever James said, it wasn't Daniel's business.

She nodded. "*Jah*, everything is good. I told James we would not be courting."

Daniel turned to face her. "You did?"

She nodded once.

A strange feeling flooded him. If he didn't know better, he'd label it relief. But that was ridiculous. Fannie was a coworker, a competent nurse and midwife. They delivered babies together; that was all. He was merely relieved that Fannie's attention would no longer be divided between her work and James's efforts to court her.

He cleared his throat and looked around for something else to talk about. He pointed to a line of animals wandering through town. "I guess the livestock is moving home." With fences and barns down, the survivors had run until they were exhausted. Now goats, horses, cows, and other animals were coming out of their temporary shelters. They'd pause to eat the grass still visible then meander on toward their homes. The sheer numbers were a sight to behold.

"They have the instinct to go home." Fannie watched the parade. "I wonder if I'll find Frieda's milk cow."

"So what do we do after a storm like this?" He was curious if she remembered their conversation in the rocks.

"Get some more sleep. Under two blankets." Fannie

shivered. "I still can't get rid of the cold shivering over me."

"We were miserable, yes, but we are also fortunate. It could have been worse. Your horse and buggy were okay, and so was my truck. Our families are all alive and well." He wasn't sure where the positive thoughts sprang from, given the destruction surrounding them. Yes, it could have been worse. They could have been caught in the mudslide, their bodies still buried. But his sudden lighter spirit was out of proportion to that escape days ago. He felt like running and gamboling like a newborn sheep. But he kept his feet firmly planted.

Fannie was silent for a moment then let out a breath. "I've been thinking…I'm sorry for stopping."

"What do you mean?" Daniel had no idea what she meant but didn't want her to think he didn't remember something that was obviously important to her.

"When I asked you to stop walking and stay with me at the cave." She shook her head. "That was selfish of me. We could have gotten home much sooner if not for the time we spent in there."

"Not necessarily. There was lightning, high water, and no one around to help." He smiled for good measure. "Stopping was the right thing to do. We had more energy, and the rain had lessened."

"Thanks. I needed to hear that." Her smile told him they were on good terms.

"And if you felt as tired as I was, you have no reason to apologize."

Fannie stopped and pointed up. "Look."

He lifted his hand over his eyes to see the most beautiful rainbow he'd ever seen.

Beautiful bands of color arched and stretched through the sky.

God had not forgotten them. Indeed.

Chapter Twenty-Eight

Daniel parked his car in front of the hospital. He was fifteen minutes late. He'd never been late since he started working there. Until today.

Memories of the storm and of his time with Fannie kept rushing through his mind. Was it the ferocious mud and rain or simply her presence that made the whole thing so unforgettable?

And then there was his tremor. It had been changing, that was sure, but he'd thought with some therapy it might get better. And it might have, if he spent time doing the physical therapy, but that hadn't happened. So here he was, giving himself the same advice he gave others. Rest. Exercise. Eat right. Take time to relax.

As he walked through the hospital door he wondered if this tremor would cost him his job. How much longer could he continue to treat clients when he had issues of his own?

The vow he made to treat his patients circled around his mind. Was this thing going to go away? Should he tell the chief of staff? Was he overreacting?

And then there was Jack. Yeah, Daniel would ask

Jack's advice. As much of a rake as he was, Jack was a good doctor.

Walking through the hallways he felt vulnerable, as if everyone knew and was staring at his arm, hoping to see something. But this had been slowly coming for a long time now.

A slap to the back caught his attention.

"Where have you been, besides saving the Amish?" Jack walked in front of him with a sly look on his face.

"How did you know I was in the community?" Daniel was more than surprised. He'd asked his nurse to cover for him but that was it, and he was away much longer than planned.

"Everybody knows if you're not here you're probably with the Amish. And after the news reports about how hard that area was hit, you're famous, man." Jack's comments were always exaggerated.

"The community was hit hard, but it could have been worse. I just treated a few people for exhaustion, exposure, cuts, and bruises." For just a moment he felt a surge of competition. "You were probably here, saving trauma victims." He let out a breath and started walking. Jack fell in beside him.

For the first time he didn't feel confident that he could perform his job. But he needed to do well at the hospital today. Then he'd take a few days of true vacation. Relax. Do some arm exercises. Get past this.

"Where are you? I just asked you two questions and you went blank." Jack shook his head.

"'I have a lot on my mind."

"I can see that. What happened to you out there?"

"Nothing we couldn't handle."

"You make it seem easy. Wish the Amish would let us in to see what was going on."

"There was a lot of mud damage but no loss of life." They walked down the hall toward the changing rooms. But Daniel didn't want to talk about what happened that night, not yet anyway.

Jack scoffed. "So you're giving me the official statement too?"

Daniel stopped and turned to him. "There's nothing else anyone needs to know. This wasn't anything other than a storm that a lot of people got caught in."

Jack stared at him. "But two people from the Amish community died. That's a pretty big deal."

Anxiety rushed in as Daniel searched his memory for anyone he hadn't seen after the storm.

"You all right?" Jack looked over at him and tilted his head.

"This is the first I've heard of any fatalities." Names and faces swirled in his mind. Who lost their lives that day?

"Sorry, Daniel. I figured you were just holding back, trying not to sound like a hero." He shrugged.

"Yeah, no. Umm, you surprised me." He thought everyone had been accounted for.

"I didn't realize the storm was that ferocious, plus I spent most of the night in a cave."

"Daniel." Cindy's voice sounded behind him, and he closed his eyes. She was the last person he was ready to talk with.

"Hi." He took a step back.

"I'm glad you're okay." She tilted her head to one side as if studying him.

"Did you know the people who died?" Flashes of his mother, father, and siblings rolled around and stopped on one face. Fannie. Then he felt guilty.

Someone was mourning the loss of a loved one, and all he could think about was how glad he was that his family was safe. That Fannie was safe. She was all he seemed to think about lately.

Both Jack's and Cindy's brows were knit in confusion.

He wondered what expression he must be wearing and forced a smile.

Jack shook his head. "I'll catch you later." Jack waved and walked away as quickly as he could. Now the awkward conversation with Cindy would begin.

"What was that all about?" She watched Jack walk away and turned back to Daniel, who took an extra beat before looking at her.

He shrugged and shook his head.

"Sounds like you had quite a time with that storm." Her words were gentle, but her eyes told a different story. They held censure and disappointment, which he deserved. As much as he wanted to make things work with her, it didn't seem to be possible. And after spending time with Fannie and helping in the community, he knew who he truly wanted. But they couldn't have a future together. They lived in different worlds.

"Daniel?"

Her voice brought him back. "Sorry. I just remembered something."

"Which means you're too busy to talk?" She folded her arms and gave him a glare. She had every right to be irritated with him.

"Listen, I owe you an apology. A lot happened during

that storm and my head's still there with the Amish rebuilding their homes." Maybe that was lame but it was the truth, and he hoped she'd understand that. Even if not, he'd explained all he could.

She took a minute and then nodded. "I can see that." She lifted her brows and waited for his reply.

"I'll do what I can, when I can. That's my honest answer." He hoped that was enough. If not, he'd done as much as possible for now.

Chapter Twenty-Nine

Fannie stood in the hospital hallway watching Daniel and Cindy converse. She couldn't hear their conversation, but she saw the way Cindy looked at Daniel.

Fannie hadn't liked Cindy the day she met her and liked her even less now. But Cindy knew a side of Daniel that she didn't. She thought there were feelings growing between them, but seeing him back in the hospital with his friends made her wonder if she'd been wrong. She gave an audible gulp.

Daniel turned around. His eyes lit up. "Hey, I didn't see you there. Have you been here long?" He looked at Cindy who grimaced, turned on her heel, and strode away.

Fannie shrugged. She didn't know what to do or think so she just let Daniel do the talking.

"I hear the water level has gone down and most of the houses are livable again." He waited for a reply, but she was still thinking of what to say.

"Things are getting back to normal." Except them. But there was no them, she just realized for the first time.

"I've got to get back into the swing of things back here."

He took a phone from his shirt pocket and checked the messages.

She smoothed her hair into her *kapp*. "*Jah*, me too." She meant it in more ways than he knew.

"Where are you headed?" He reached for her, but she moved away. This was not the place for her, and she was needed at home so that's where she would stay.

"I'll be by the community when I get off."

"I'll be there." She almost felt guilty knowing she would do nothing of the sort. He was with someone, and she was just…well, she wasn't as important to him as he was to her. Best to leave it at that.

"Wait." He looked up from his phone. "Why did you come here? Is someone hurt? What can I do for you?"

She forced a smile. "I was…well, I wanted to see you and tell you that everyone is doing better, and we understand that you're busy here and can't give us as much time."

His face fell. "You're telling me not to come?"

She nodded. "*Jah.* Please don't come back. It's too—" She whirled away and hurried for the exit, her skirt flapping around her legs.

When she walked out the hospital doors she let out a breath and squared her shoulders. She had work to do. There was still enough cleanup to do to keep her busy, not to mention the regular chores.

Almost as soon as she stepped outside, she spotted Alice, a woman who drove the Amish to places they weren't able to get to easily in their buggies. She'd given her a ride to the hospital, but since Fannie told her she'd be a while, so Fannie was surprised to see Alice waiting.

"You're done already? I had been talking to a friend,

but I was just about to leave." She rested her arm on the steering wheel and looked through the passenger window.

Fannie nodded and climbed in the back seat.

"You going home?" She gave Fannie a quick look then started the car.

Fannie nodded. She was in no mood to talk but appreciated the ride. Sometimes she wished she could drive, just to get somewhere faster, but she forced herself to be content with the occasional ride.

"Are you okay?" Alice draped her arm over the back of the passenger's side and her small dog poked his head over the seat. He sniffed the air in Fannie's direction, then disappeared again.

Fannie sighed deeply and let Alice do the driving and talking. "Doc and you have a problem?" She kept her eyes on the road.

Fannie gave up. "How do you know these things?" It wasn't the first time Alice knew what to say, but it made her feel exposed at times.

"Cab drivers are like bartenders; they console and listen thorough hard times." She looked at Fannie in the rearview mirror. "I also heard you told James Miller to stop courting you."

Fannie grimaced. "*Jah.*" And didn't she feel foolish now, hurting James because she thought she and Daniel had something. Should she go talk to James, apologize, and ask him to call again?

She shook her head no. Even if she'd imagined Daniel developing feelings for her, she knew she had no feelings for James. He would recover from his heartache and find someone else. It appeared *Mamm* was right: no man would put up with Fannie.

Fannie turned to the window and watched the miles go by. But that just made her sad. As they got closer to her community, the debris became more consistent.

"It's not easy to see, but it looks better each time I go this way." Alice glanced at her rearview mirror, and their eyes met.

"There's a reason for everything. I just wish I knew what it was." Fannie spoke more to herself than to Alice.

"You know, you have a big heart, and you did good helping the people who were in a hard way when the storm came. You should do more of that."

Fannie wasn't sure what she meant and was not in the mood to figure it out. "Do more of what?"

"Helping people. You know the hospital has candy stripers—volunteers—come in to help people who are in the hospital. You do that anyway, so why not give it a try?"

"For one reason: it takes time and money to get there and back. And to be honest, I feel like I should be helping the people in the community, not in the hospital. They already have help, medical help even. I help where I'm needed."

"Can't argue with that." Alice left it at that, and Fannie was glad for it.

She had to admit, though, if Daniel were at the hospital during her shifts, she wouldn't say no to volunteering. "Maybe I'll think about it." But if she offered help with selfish motives, wasn't that wrong? She tucked that thought away.

They rode up to the community telephone booth, and Fannie gave Alice her due and headed home. As she passed the clinic, she noticed Rebecca Bonetrager walking toward her.

"*Hallo.*" Fannie smiled.

Rebecca's breath was heavy, and Fannie could tell she was almost in tears.

"What's wrong?"

"Elton cut his hand while butchering a cow. Doc is there to try to put some stitches in but I'm just not sure..."

"Of what?"

"Is Daniel anywhere close by?" Rebecca cleared her throat, obviously worried for her husband.

"*Nee*, but I can ask Daniel to come by when I see him. But I don't know when he'll get here." Especially since she'd just told him not to come back.

"Well, to be honest, I'd rather wait for him than have Doc try to mend Elton. Is that bad of me to say?"

"*Nee*, I have to say I would think the same thing." Fannie was glad she wasn't the first to admit her lack of trust in Doc's abilities but didn't want to hurt the old man's feelings. "I think he has less patience in his older years."

They fell quiet, as if they were both deciding what they were comfortable saying next.

"I'll call Daniel." Fannie decided she'd ask him to come. "And if I don't get him, then we'll have Doc stitch him up." Fannie was glad to have made a decision, but now she wondered if it would be too much of a change of heart for Daniel. Either way, Fannie would be at Rebecca's home doing what she could as soon as she could. "Tell Doc to please wait for me to assist him, so he can teach me about stitching."

"*Jah*, that will make him wait." Rebecca turned and headed back home.

Fannie went to the community telephone and rang the hospital. She got a nurse—not Cindy—and asked her to give Daniel her message then hurried on to Elton and Rebecca's *haus*. She didn't want to wait for a call back.

Chapter Thirty

Fannie was sure her expression gave away her dismay when Cindy walked in with Daniel to help with Elton. She didn't mean for it to turn out this way but here they all were, together, with the tension between them. But what did she expect? Dismissing him from her life one minute, then calling him to come stitch up a patient less than an hour later. For it to be an official call, he had to bring a nurse. Cindy made sense. Fannie took a deep breath and forced a welcoming smile.

"We were about to call Doc back. He was exhausted after explaining stitches to me. So I wrapped up Elton's hand tight and told Doc to go home for a nap," Fannie explained.

"Sorry it took so long. We ran into some traffic." He spoke as he nodded toward the kitchen. "Hot water and clean cloths. Also a sanitizer with a cloth."

When Fannie stood and walked toward the kitchen, Cindy followed. "I'll help."

She was the last person Fannie wanted to spend time with, but there was no way out of it unless she was willing to be rude.

The click-clack of Cindy's shoes seemed louder than usual. Or perhaps it was Fannie's discomfort that made all the noises in the room echo.

Fannie found a pot to hold the water and looked for the sanitizer.

"I guess all that's left is the cloth Daniel wanted. Unless you want to do that too." Cindy's smile tipped to the side as she waited for Fannie's response.

"I think I have everything." She wanted to say more but that would get her nowhere. And the more she thought about it, Daniel and Cindy were a better fit. Their lifestyles, their jobs, where they lived—the list went on.

Cindy took a cloth from a drawer. "I'm not giving up on him." Her gaze met Fannie's.

"He grew up in the community; he understands us." Even though she wished he didn't. This woman was closer to his current lifestyle. Yet there was something about him that made her think he missed being here.

She left the kitchen before Cindy could reply.

"Elton, are you ready for this?" Daniel asked as he cleaned his hands then handed the bowl to Fannie. He paused and held his hand out, obviously realizing he had one patient and two nurses.

Fannie saw it coming and prepared to hand him the tools he needed. They had worked together before, and the country ways were probably different from what Cindy was used to.

"*Jah*, this isn't the first or the last time for me."

"Good. It's my first time, so you tell me if I do anything wrong," Daniel said teasingly.

Elton chortled.

Cindy watched as Daniel and Fannie worked together,

with Fannie passing him what he needed before he asked. After the first half hour of stitching, Cindy stood. "I guess you don't need me after all." She left.

After twenty-four stitches and an hour of work, all was well.

"There's something to be said about a country doctor." Elton looked at his hand. "Are you going to stay here for a while, Doctor? I'd like to pay you for your time. You might like some steak for your trouble." He winced as Rebecca glared at him.

"When you're up to it, I'd be glad to take some steaks. What you can do for me now is to let your hand heal and use the salve I put on that injury. And no more butchering for a while."

Elton nodded. Daniel hadn't looked so happy in a long time—a very long time. Fannie met Daniel's gaze, and she quickly busied herself, picking up the cloths and bits of bandages. Daniel wondered what she was thinking.

When Daniel walked out the door, Fannie was right behind him. He stopped and turned her way. "Something wrong?" He expected the worst and started to turn back to the house.

"No. Well, yes." She looked down at his hand and quietly asked, "The tremors are acting up again, aren't they, Daniel?"

His breath left his body in a whoosh. A part of him was almost glad to be able to tell someone. But another part knew he couldn't delay telling his supervisor. And that would be the hard thing. The hospital was his real job. It paid the bills, unlike his work with the Amish, who appreciated his practice but sometimes paid him with meat and garden produce.

"I… didn't realize it was that noticeable." He stared at her since there was nothing to hide now. "How long have you known?"

"A while, but I thought you had it under control." She glanced down at his hand that had the tremor. "I'm sorry, Daniel, but should you be practicing at the hospital? I mean, for your own sake as well as the patients'?"

"I can't answer that. Only the higher ups can make that decision." He stopped and turned to her. "I don't want you part of this. It's time to get it out in the open. I almost feel better about working out there." He pointed in the direction of Amish country. "Less to worry about and good patients."

She whipped her head toward him. "Would you do that?"

"I don't know if I would live with the rules again, but I do enjoy spending time with the Amish, my first home. But it's not about me. It's the community. I left long ago, and the bishop wasn't happy about that."

"He shouldn't have the authority to be the bishop, or at least not to make decisions that affect whole families." She crossed her arms and let out a breath.

"Fannie, that's not like you. You feel strongly about this."

"It's not just me. The old man had lost his faculties… if only someone would stand up to him and insist he step down."

"That's like asking the pope to leave the Vatican." He grinned, but she didn't. It wasn't the first time he'd heard criticism of the bishop, and it wouldn't be the last, he was sure. "But you just don't do that, unless you have a good reason. This kind of talk might be considered divisive, given how strict and unaware the bishop running things here is."

"That's it, though. The deacons and others with power do most everything now because of his neglect of important matters." She gripped both her elbows so tightly her knuckles were white.

"Now that you mention it, I do remember some grumbles going around when things started to change with the bishop. This is interesting information. I'm just not sure what I can do with it. He is still the one in charge."

She scoffed. "That's a surprise, coming from you. Since when do you care what the bishop says?"

He looked into her green eyes. "You care about the community, and he's still part of it. I don't think you'd want to give up stitching or quilting with the ladies because the bishop tells them to steer clear of you."

She grinned. "How do you know I like to quilt?" She was surprised he'd noticed her on those rare times he came into the community for something not medically related. He had been watching her.

He lifted his eyes to meet hers and smiled. He hoped to get over his feelings for her, but they seemed to be going in a completely different direction than he expected.

Chapter Thirty-One

"Doc's gone sick and there are some still hurt from that landslide. I know it's a lot to ask but can you help us out here?"

Daniel held his breath when he heard Fannie's request over the phone line. He knew where he wanted to be but that wouldn't go over well with the hospital staff. The best he could do was switch shifts with someone. He'd been doing that a lot though, even before the issues that cropped up before and after the storm.

"It would be nice if they could come to me."

"Some could, but that's not possible for many of them."

"Let me ask around and see if I can trade some shifts."

"*Danke*, Daniel. You know I wouldn't ask unless we needed you." She hung up.

Her request alone was enough to get him there. Now he just needed to find a trade to cover his shift. The first person he ran across was Cindy. She wasn't scheduled as his assistant according to the board. That would make things easier. She'd covered for him before when he needed to make an emergency trip to the community. He wasn't sure what was going on with them, but the more he thought about it he couldn't decide if they could ever have a relationship or if they were just compatible as friends and coworkers.

Daniel made his rounds and managed to convince a third-year resident to stay on call for him. He left the hospital an hour and a half after his conversation with Fannie. The drive seemed unusually long and a bit lonely.

He parked in front of the schoolhouse just as Fannie instructed. The lane was crowded with buggies and waiting horses.

He hurried inside.

Fannie's voice was one among several that echoed through the room. He stopped and stood for a moment, deciphering who were the healthy Amish caring for those in need.

He made his way over to Fannie. Seeing the makeshift hospital made awe grow in his chest. There were clearly more injured than they could fit in the clinic. She'd done all this for the injured and ill?

Some had cuts and bruises. Others were sick, possibly from the still unclean water. He thought the community was doing well after the storm. He'd assumed too much; they were still struggling.

Fannie met his eyes and motioned for him to follow her. They made their way to a small sitting area in a corner of the large room. A hickory rocker with a braided rug sat next to a potbelly stove. It was a place for the helpers to rest, he presumed.

A young girl played with a baby doll nearby. She looked up and her face sprouted a smile.

"Lydia!" He stopped himself from embracing her. "What are you doing here?"

"Mrs. Lapp is helping. She brought Miriam and Lydia. The older folks enjoy seeing the young ones." Fannie answered for the mute child.

"How are things going?" he asked. An obvious question with an obvious answer, but he was surprised at how efficient they were.

"We still have a way to go, but we're making good progress. We need you for the more difficult situations, like this mother-to-be that we're guessing is breach."

"Right up my alley." He bent down to whisper to Lydia. "I'll see you after I finish some work."

She nodded and returned to her doll.

Daniel stood. "Lead me to her." His confidence waned after just a moment though. He held up his hand. When no shaking started, he followed Fannie to a cot against the far wall. A quilt was strung around her to give her a semblance of privacy. He sat down next to the mother-to-be.

"This is Annie Fisher." Fannie made the introduction.

A young woman with dark circles under her eyes gazed up at him. She smiled wanly. "Dr. Kauffman, I'm so glad you're here with my baby. Are there any problems?"

Fannie motioned for him to answer so he obliged. "I hear your baby might be breach."

"Is that what you think too?" Her face contorted with worry, and he knew she would need extra help.

"Either way I'm sure you and your baby will be fine, unless you've noticed anything out of the norm?"

She shook her head and let out a breath. "That's what they said, but I wanted to hear it from you."

"Let's keep Fannie in here with us." Fannie was better

with the worriers, and he just wanted her by his side for just about anything these days.

She patted Annie's hand. "You know Dr. Kauffman is one of the best around. You're in good hands."

Annie took a breath, and when he did the exam, she seemed much more relaxed.

But what Fannie watched was Daniel's unsteady hand.

He cleared his throat. "It does look like a breach. We'll keep an eye on the babe."

She held out a hand. "*Danke*, Dr. Kauffman."

"You're welcome." He stood and followed Fannie to treat a few more patients. Before they knew it, the patients who needed the most care were all but taken care of.

Daniel went to those with serious problems. Fannie checked on the ones who had less severe needs or who just liked someone of the Amish way to tend to them.

Between the two of them they ended up with a lot of patients successfully treated.

"You've done a lot here today considering you're used to the luxuries of a hospital. But then I knew you would." She glanced down, as if trying to decide if she should say something to him about his hand. Her gaze strayed to his hand again, but it was steady.

"If we're done here, I should get back home to get some sleep before tomorrow's shift. That is, unless you need something more. Mrs. Fisher isn't in labor yet, so the baby could still turn on his own."

She nodded distractedly.

"Fannie, what is it? What's wrong?" He followed her gaze to where she was looking. He was holding his bad hand without realizing it. He let go.

"Daniel, you trust me...don't you?"

"Of course I do, Fannie. I know my limitations."

"What about the hospital?" Her voice was small and timid and most un-Fannie-like.

He shook his head. "It's something I have to work through. This isn't the time or the place to talk about it." He stuck his hands in his pockets. "Just for the record, I've never done anything I didn't think I could handle. I hope you know that."

With that he turned and walked through the room without speaking or waving good-bye.

Fannie watched Daniel stride from the room, brushing past a couple in the doorway as he exited.

They were dressed in Amish garb, but the woman's hair, long and lank, straggled past her shoulders. She was young, more girl than woman. The man gripped a battered hat in one hand while his other hand beat a staccato rhythm against his leg. Fannie watched as the pair surveyed the room.

The woman gripped the man's arm and pointed. Fannie followed the gesture.

Her heart lurched. *It couldn't be.*

The woman was pointing at Lydia, still playing contentedly with her doll.

The pair made their way toward the little girl.

Fannie strode to intersect their path before they reached the child. She slipped between chairs and stepped into the makeshift aisle in front of them.

"Can I help you?" she asked, blocking their way.

"Our little girl," the man said. "We lost her in the storm."

Fannie's forehead creased. "I—"

The woman brushed past her and rushed to Lydia.

"Misty, my baby!" She clutched Lydia to her chest.

Lydia struggled to get away. Panic covered her face.

Fannie hurried to Lydia, and she hurled herself toward Fannie and clutched her skirts.

"Misty, what's wrong, baby? Papa and I have been looking everywhere for you. Why did you run off in that storm? I know the lightning frightened you, but we wouldn't let anything hurt you." The words tumbled from the woman's lips like a rehearsed speech.

Fannie kept a firm hold on Lydia. "She doesn't seem to want to go with you."

The man stood by his wife's side. "I'm Jonah Troyer. This here is my wife Sarah. That's our child. Thank *ye* kindly for taking care of her, but we'll be going now." He reached for Lydia's hand, but she buried her face in Fannie's skirts.

Fannie clutched Lydia close and stared at the couple. The man—the father?—swiped his middle finger under his nose. "Her name is Misty."

Fannie scanned them from head to toe. "Misty isn't a traditional Amish name."

"Yes…we—she was born on a foggy evening so we named her Misty."

Mrs. Troyer nodded.

Fannie made a decision. "I'll call Social Services."

The woman's eyes widened. The man shook his head. "No reason for that. She's our Misty."

Fannie waved at Mrs. Lapp, who approached them. "Would you please call Social Services?"

"Social Services?" Mrs. Lapp's gaze traveled from Lydia to Fannie to the strange couple.

Fannie nodded. "Yes. We'll wait for the social worker to get here."

"I say there—" Mr. Troyer objected.

Fannie silenced him with a look. "You may wait out front until the social worker arrives and then we will talk."

He gave his wife a look. Her lips tightened but she gave one short nod.

They had to wait a long time for the social worker. Fannie kept busy, checking on her patients. Lydia and Miriam played on the hook rug. Mrs. Lapp helped Fannie write down patients' names and symptoms. But Fannie kept a close eye on Lydia and her so-called "parents." They seemed content to sit near Lydia and send her an occasional glance.

Fannie pursed her lips. How could this couple be Lydia's real parents? And even if they were who they claimed to be, Lydia had been part of the community since before the storm. And these people said they lost their Misty in the storm. There were too many questions for Fannie to just hand Lydia over to a pair of complete strangers.

Finally Mrs. Wurtemberg arrived. She bustled in, a blur of gray—gray hair, gray skirt, gray sweater. Her manner, though, was as bright and sunny as a June day.

"So, what do we have here?" She paused at Fannie's side, watching Lydia and Miriam.

Mr. and Mrs. Troyer stood.

Fannie nodded to them. "They say Lydia is theirs, that she ran off in the storm and her name is Misty."

Mrs. Wurtemberg's brow furrowed. "That's an unusual name for an Amish child, isn't it? And Lydia arrived before the storm."

"That's why we called you." Fannie folded her arms, prepared to glare a warning if the couple tried to approach Lydia.

But they appeared harmless. Just another young Amish couple. A bit straggly in appearance, but that could be due to the recent storm and upheaval.

They clutched each other's hands, another thing unusual since most Amish didn't hold with public displays of affection.

Fannie made the introductions. Mrs. Wurtemberg turned to her. "Is there some place quiet and more private where we can discuss this?"

"Perhaps." Fannie nodded toward the small area she had curtained off to serve as a secluded examining room.

"That'll do. Mrs. Lapp," Mrs. Wurtemberg called to Lydia's foster mother, "could you please join us?"

Mrs. Lapp nodded and followed Mrs. Wurtemberg and the Troyers. Fannie watched them go. She yearned to trail after them, to listen through the hanging quilts. But no matter how attached she'd grown to Lydia, she had no rights and no say where Lydia was concerned.

The next hour passed quickly as Fannie moved from one patient to the next. Between wondering about Daniel and fretting about Lydia, she was exhausted as the last family drifted out and to their buggy. She sagged into the rocking chair next to Lydia and Miriam. They'd tired of their doll game and now their heads were bent over a puzzle.

The quilts parted, and Mrs. Wurtemberg emerged, followed by Mrs. Lapp and the Troyers.

"No." Fannie stood.

Mrs. Wurtemberg shook her head. "I have no choice."

Mrs. Lapp dashed tears from her eyes.

"Come on, Misty," Mrs. Troyer crowed. "We're going home."

"But..." Fannie stared at Mrs. Wurtemberg in horror.

Mr. Troyer bent and scooped up Lydia into his arms. Her cry of outrage pierced Fannie's heart.

"Thank *ye* for taking care of our girl." Mrs. Troyer hurried after her husband as he strode through the schoolhouse and out the door. Lydia's cries echoed in the stillness they left behind.

Fannie wrestled down the panic in her chest and chased after them. But Mrs. Wurtemberg grasped her elbow. "You have to let her go."

"How could you do that?" Fannie had to fight back tears.

Mrs. Wurtemberg sighed. "I wish I had another option. They had proof that Lydia—I mean, Misty—is their daughter. They had a birth certificate and pictures of her as a baby and a toddler."

"But she was so obviously neglected when she arrived," Fannie protested. "And they said she ran off in the storm."

Mrs. Wurtemberg's lips thinned. "They didn't say that to me." She scribbled a note on the file folder she held. "They don't live in the community. But I have their address, and I assured them I'd be following up to be certain Misty was being taken care of."

Fannie walked with Mrs. Wurtemberg to the door. Instead of watching Lydia leave in a buggy, though, a dusty blue car, missing a rear bumper, rumbled down the lane.

Chapter Thirty-Two

Daniel walked behind the shuffling coroner. He'd been asked to look at some bodies, to see if they might be Amish. If they only knew how difficult it would be for him, looking for hints—hair color, height—to see if an unidentified victim might be from his old community. How could he stand it? And then to go back and break someone's heart?

Even though it was brutal, he took special care with what he was doing now. He knew so many of them . . . he almost changed his mind. But the news would hurt more coming from *Englischers*. So no matter how hard it would be, he would do it.

His life was suddenly complicated. The people he grew up with intersected with the new life he'd built. He was now the doctor he always wanted to be. But he was no longer Amish.

He followed the coroner into the morgue and stopped at the first gurney. He drew a deep breath as Dr. Morgan lowered the sheet. Daniel shook his head. They moved to the next victim.

Ten minutes later he breathed a sigh of relief. He didn't recognize anyone in the morgue.

"Were there more Amish lost, other than the two?" he asked.

The grumpy coroner turned to him with saggy bags under his eyes and rubbed his balding head. "There are just the two that we know of."

Daniel guessed that was all he was going to get out of the man. He'd go to Jack if he needed more information. He'd asked him to keep him informed but hadn't heard from him for a while. Maybe it was a good time to stop in and see him.

"Thank you for your time, sir." Dr. Morgan turned and lifted a hand to Daniel then took a slow, tired walk back toward his office.

At that moment Daniel decided he would not live a life that didn't make his and those around him better. It gave him a lift, thinking about doing and saying some things he needed to take care of. He might even do a little forgiving along the way. His hand trembled, as if on cue after the enlightening conversation he'd had with himself.

"Hand bothering you?" Jack asked as Daniel walked into his office. He swiveled around in his chair and twined his fingers together. Daniel didn't realize he had noticed.

"It comes and goes. Thanks for asking." He copied Jack's tone. "So what's going on?"

"You tell me. You're the one who's been gone. I'd think your vacation days would be gone by now."

"The community needed a little more time after the storm. Still do actually." He studied Jack. Why didn't he understand the magnitude of this storm's impact on the community as a whole? "Maybe you just need to be there to understand all that happened and the impact it's had."

Jack shrugged. "Probably like here, right? Just a different venue."

Daniel exhaled a frustrated sigh. "We aren't going to get anywhere with this so maybe I'll come by another time." He was more than irritated.

Jack grimaced. "This is no good." He shook his head.

"What's got you riled up?" Daniel asked. Jack's irritation seemed out of proportion to Daniel taking a few hours off to take care of patients in the community.

"It's been a jungle out there. Short on staff, overreactions to news. There was almost a stampede at the grocery store. People thought there was a food shortage, which was a completely false issue. I could go on..."

"I see what you mean. I didn't realize it had gone that far. I assumed things were worse in the community due to the elevated water level." This conversation would get them nowhere, but it was an awakening to their different priorities. Neither was right or wrong, they just were.

Daniel stood and offered a hand. "Good to see you, my friend."

"And you." Jack took his time standing and looked Daniel in the eyes as they shook hands. "You know, I've never seen so many people come to support one another like the Amish have. There's just something about them that makes you want live in their shoes, just to see if it's all as good as it seems."

"I couldn't agree with you more." Daniel grinned.

Jack chuckled. "Yeah, I guess you'd know."

As Daniel left the room he had a feeling things might

change between him and Jack in the future. But that was out of his hands so he'd leave it to think about another day.

As Daniel left the hospital, he noticed the two small crosses in the garden behind the main building. They were in memory of the two who passed away in the landslide. More would be added as bodies were identified.

His heart was conflicted, wondering where he was supposed to be and why. Practice medicine or be Amish? That had always been his dilemma and why the bishop gave him the ultimatum when Daniel decided to get more education.

Doc Reuben mostly taught himself how to treat patients with herbs and his own concoctions, but Daniel wanted more. He couldn't help his inquisitive mind. God had given him a quick intelligence and the ability to learn and the discipline to thrive while studying medicine. Going to med school had been the easier dilemma. Now there was another question: Which world did he belong in?

A voice intruded on his thoughts.

"What are you doing here?" Cindy stood nearby. She took three steps closer then followed his gaze. She swallowed hard.

"I still work here. Sometimes. How are you?" He spoke mildly, not wanting to antagonize another friend.

"It's been pretty hectic. But not as hard as what you went through. That storm had to have been rough, for all of you."

He pointed to the crosses. "This is nice."

She tipped her head. "Is it? Makes me too sad." She looked away. "Did you know them?"

He grunted. "No, I didn't recognize them. They may not have been from the community. They may have been passing through."

"I suppose so. Do you know how old they were?"

He paused and tried not to get irritated. Even if she was in her nurse mode, this wasn't the time for a post-mortem debriefing. He ran a hand through his head. "Why are you asking?"

She was silent for a moment and then turned away. "No matter what the cause, I know it's hard to lose someone, especially someone young."

He folded his arms. "It's never easy."

She spoke so softly at first he thought he'd misheard. "I lost someone close to me. I figure that's why I decided to be a nurse."

Daniel let his hands drop to his sides. His left hand started to tremble, and he stuck it in his pocket. "You made the right choice. You're a good nurse, and I've seen you with the really sick and terminal. You have a special gift."

She glanced from his eyes to his hand. Did the tremor still show? He didn't want to look at it and draw even more attention to it.

Finally Cindy smiled and lifted her head a little higher. "I've got to go." She strode away as Daniel watched.

Cindy never looked back.

Chapter Thirty-Three

Fannie held the receiver in one hand and stared at the telephone. She'd been there ten minutes already but couldn't bring herself to call Daniel.

He'd been frustrated and angry with her when he left the other day. But he loved Lydia, and Fannie knew he would be angrier if she didn't tell him about Lydia's parents taking her back.

Fannie drew a deep breath then dialed Daniel's mobile phone.

"Hello?" He sounded wary, as if not sure who or what would be on the other end of the line.

"Daniel." Her throat closed, and she couldn't get out anything more.

"Fannie? What's wrong?" The wariness was gone and replaced by concern.

His care opened the floodgates to her heart and the tears fell freely now. "Oh, Daniel. She's gone."

"What? Who's gone? Is Frieda okay?"

She nodded forgetting he couldn't see her response.

"Fannie, what's going on? Who—"

"Lydia," Fannie managed to choke out. "It's Lydia. Her parents..."

"No," Daniel breathed.

"I'm sorry. They came and took her. The social worker said they had proof she was theirs. Her name is Misty."

"But how?"

"They said she ran off in the storm. But that's a lie. They don't live in the community either. Something's wrong, Daniel. I know it."

"Did you get their names?"

"Jonah and Sarah Troyer. They were dressed Amish, but not quite, if that makes sense. Sarah's hair wasn't in a *kapp*, and Jonah didn't seem to know how to wear his hat. And Amish couples don't name their daughter Misty."

"I'm going to do some checking. I'll let you know what I find out."

"*Danke*, Daniel."

"And Fannie?" He cleared his throat.

"*Jah*?"

"I'm sorry for leaving the way I did the other day."

Her lips lifted in a smile. "I'm sorry if it seemed I was doubting you or your skills."

"No, you were right to question me. I'm... being tested to see what's wrong, why I have this tremor."

"I'm glad," she whispered.

"I'll do some checking on the Troyers and then will be in touch. Thank you for calling me."

"You're welcome."

She hung up and stared into space.

Daniel had barely hung up with Fannie when his phone rang again. "Hello? Fannie?" He shoved aside the newspaper he'd been reading at his small kitchen table.

"Fannie? No, it's Jack. Listen, I only have a minute, but I heard a rumor about you."

"Me?" His coffee cup rattled as he set it on the table.

"I heard that human resources told the chief of staff that you now owe the hospital for all the time you've been taking off. And he's not happy about it."

"That's all? I can easily make up the time with a couple of weekend rotations in the ER."

"That's not all." Jack's voice lowered. "I heard talk about your hand tremor."

Daniel sat back in the chair like he'd been sucker punched. "What?"

"That's all I know. I don't want you to be blindsided if you get a call from the chief."

"Thanks, Jack." He hung up and sat stunned. He knew he was running out of time. The hospital would want him there, seeing patients. He knew that, even agreed that was where he should be. So why did that feel like a death sentence? Why did he feel like he belonged in the community, taking care of Amish patients? And now Fannie's news about Lydia gnawed at him. Something was wrong there, and he'd promised to look into it.

"Well, word sure gets around." Daniel spoke to himself. He had a couple ideas of who must have tattled about his hand tremor. He didn't think anyone but Fannie and Jack and maybe Cindy had noticed it. Perhaps he hadn't hidden it as well as he thought. Oh well. As they said, it was usually the last person you'd think.

A knock on the door took his thoughts away.

He opened the door to see a courier with an envelope in his hand.

"Daniel Kauffman?"

"That's me." He almost sounded cheerful. Considering everything else that had gone wrong lately, why not something else to go with it?

The young man thrust the envelope at him.

Daniel took it and stared.

"Please sign here."

Daniel signed and waved the guy off.

The courier turned to go, but paused and spoke over his shoulder.

"Wait, there's another courier behind me."

Daniel rubbed his eyes wishing he were dreaming instead of wide awake and standing on his front stoop, getting continual bad news. He accepted the second envelope then returned to his kitchen table. Both had the hospital's return address.

He sipped his coffee and stared at them.

It seemed like overkill for the hospital to deliver its official paperwork this way, but he knew this was their standard procedure. At least one of them would be from human resources. Thanks to Jack's heads-up call, he knew that was coming. The second envelope was the puzzle.

He sighed and set down his coffee mug. Just staring at them wasn't going to make them go away.

He ripped open the first envelope, pulled out the single page, and scanned it.

As he expected, his vacation and sick days were down to nothing. Effective immediately, if he took off any more time, it would be without pay.

Then he opened the second one to see the notice he didn't want, about his tremor. As he feared, he couldn't treat patients until he was diagnosed and the tremor subsided.

He drew a stabbing breath. He'd thought he was so good at hiding it that no one else noticed. Or maybe he'd been given a free pass. But he'd not thought about his patients. He owed it to them to be at his best. How could he suture up a cut if he couldn't stop his own hand from shaking? He couldn't.

After taking a good look at himself, he was pretty disgusted at the egotistical and arrogant person he'd become. It had happened so gradually, he hadn't even noticed.

And now he wanted to do something to keep busy, but he was barred from working. He'd be making no money at all. His only pay would be the vegetables and canned goods his Amish patients paid him.

He rubbed his eyes and fought the longing for the one place he felt accepted.

Well, why not? What was keeping him here?

He hurried to pack a few things.

The first stop would be to see his mom. There was nothing better than unconditional love. And some cherry pie. Mom was real good at both.

An image of Lydia, lost, dirty, and forlorn popped into his head.

Perhaps, his *mamm* would be his second stop.

He locked up the house and hurried to the truck. He

had the right clothes to blend in for a while, and if not, someone would offer him something.

But before heading to the community, he aimed for an apartment building on the outskirts of town.

He'd been invited there for dinner or coffee many times. He'd gone twice. A loose community of ex-Amish lived in the area. Like Daniel, they missed their families and farms, but for various reasons had been placed under the *Meidung*—the shunning. Daniel wasn't shunned because he'd left for school before being baptized into the faith.

If anyone knew about this Troyer couple—"Amish, but not quite"—according to Fannie, it would be someone in this apartment building.

He left the truck parked at the curb and climbed the front steps. He examined the call buttons for the right name. There. He stabbed the small circle by the label that read Luthy.

"Who is it?" A voice, pleasant though disembodied, drifted through the speaker.

"It's Daniel Kauffman."

Silence met his announcement.

Then a buzzer sounded, and he pushed through the door.

He climbed the cement steps to the second floor and then made his way to the door labeled B3. The center courtyard of the building had some feeble grass and a sand box. All the apartments were reached by a walkway that circled the courtyard.

He started to knock, but before he drew his knuckles back, the door swung open and he was engulfed in a hug.

"*Ach*, Daniel! It's been so long." Patience Luthy thrust

him back and gazed at him from head to toes. "You look tired. Are you working too hard again?"

He smiled. "It's good to see you too. I'm sorry for not staying in touch better."

"Come in, I have coffee ready." Her light-colored hair was pulled in to a braid that twitched down her back as she moved through the small apartment.

She led him to a neat table in the little alcove off her kitchen. He sat while she bustled around gathering sugar and pouring milk into a small ceramic cow with a spout for a nose. He'd known Patience all his life. She was about ten years older, but they'd grown up on neighboring farms. She'd left the community during her *Rumspringa* and decided not to go back. Like him, she wasn't shunned by her family and friends, but given her new life, she had little in common with them. She'd formed a loose circle of former Amish, some under *Meidung*, some not.

"Here." She set a coffee mug in front of him, then added a plate with sugar cookies. She settled into her chair and folded her hands under her chin. "Spill. To what do I owe the pleasure of your company?"

He took a sip and smiled at her over his cup. "I need information."

"In return I need news of my family. I know you've been making visits to the community, delivering babies, seeing patients."

How Patience still managed to keep such close tabs on her former life mystified Daniel. "Can't whoever tells you what I'm up to also tell you about your family?"

She shook her head. "I never reveal my sources." She grinned and winked. "So anything you tell me is confidential."

He cast his mind back to his last visit, combing his memory for something to tell her. "I'm in the process of chopping down the old dead tree in my *mamm's* yard. Even after the storm it's still hanging in there. She said she was going to offer to share the firewood with your brother if he would help with the chopping and stacking."

Patience nodded once. "Good. Thank you. Now what do you want to know?"

"A couple named Troyer, with a young girl."

Her expression darkened, and her gaze darted from his face to the corner behind him. "Why?"

"I'm concerned about the girl."

Patience drew a deep breath and sipped from her own coffee cup. "I know who you mean."

"Where can I find them?"

She shook her head. "Not so fast. What do you know about them and the girl?"

"I know the girl ran away from them. Or they sent her away. I know she doesn't speak. I know she's been neglected, if not abused. I know she was happy living with the Lapps, and I know the Troyers don't love her like Fannie and I—I mean, not like the Lapps love her."

Patience's eyes brightened. "How is Fannie? I always liked Frieda. I hear she and her daughter-in-law bicker an awful lot, and I imagine Fannie tires of that."

Daniel leaned back in the wooden chair. "She's an excellent midwife."

"I see." Good humor danced in her eyes.

He shifted and shrugged. "Now, about the Troyers?"

Her lips tightened. "Jonah and Sarah. They're not legally married. They both grew up Amish, but left the order in their teens. They're drug users. I've been keeping an eye on them since they had Misty, making sure she was fed and clothed. They take pretty good care of her. I'd give them a few dollars for diapers when she was a baby. A couple months ago they said she went to visit her grandparents in Ohio. I had my doubts, but they said their families wanted to know their granddaughter so they'd agreed to a long visit. I know they wouldn't hurt her. Neglect yes, but not outright cruelty. So I believed them."

"She appeared in the community about then."

"Hmm..." Patience considered this. "She's been taken care of?"

He nodded. "She was happy with the Lapps. Clean and fed."

"I'll go see them." Patience stood and refilled both their coffee cups. "I'll find out if Misty is back from her grandparents' and if she might be going for another long visit."

"And you'll let me know?" he asked.

Patience's dimple showed in her right cheek. "I will."

Daniel finished his coffee, allowed Patience to hug him good-bye, then returned to the truck and headed toward the community.

The traffic was easy this time of day, in between breakfast and lunch. Mom's best meal was always at noon. If her friends were visiting, there would be even more food, and they'd be spoiling him like when he was a kid again.

As he made the turn into the community center he noticed a new sign had been put up since the storm, only now the name had been made into Mudfordville.

"Gotta love Amish creativity," he said to himself.

He glanced at his watch. Lunch wouldn't be for a

couple of hours. He had time to swing by and check on Frieda and her hip.

When Frieda opened the door and saw Daniel, she slapped a hand to her chest. "Well, if it isn't the stranger." She waddled over to him and gave him a tight hug.

"You're going to smother me."

"Where have you been? Working yourself to death I suppose." She motioned him inside and cooled herself with a nice fan. Daniel knew to comment on it.

"Did you make that fan, Frieda?" He whistled for effect.

"Oh, this old thing? She stopped fanning and admired it again.

"Too bad you and Verna don't make more for the Mudfordville auction." He looked at her out of the corner of one eye.

"Don't miss her one iota."

He waited for a moment to see how much Frieda really missed her strong daughter-in-law. He knew they cared about each other, and the tension between them had to be hard for both of the stubborn women.

"Is Fannie around?" he finally asked.

She winked as she settled herself in her rocking chair. "*Nee*, but she'll likely be back soon. Do you want to stay for lunch?" Her rocker squeaked slowly as she waited for his answer.

He shrugged. "Thanks, but I can't. Now that my *mammi* is back from Ohio, I'm going to go see her."

"She misses you, ya know." She turned toward him.

He opened his mouth to ask if she meant his *mamm* or Fannie. Then shrugged. It didn't really matter. "And I miss her. Are you going to give me grief?" He couldn't help but smile. Teasing Frieda always made him leave a little happier. "How is she?"

"She's good. We're all good, all of us, praise *Gott*." She slapped his leg so hard he made a mental note to keep himself at a distance.

"Speaking of *Gott*, when's the last time you went to church? And don't use work for an excuse." She gave him a level gaze that would have a lesser man stammering that he'd be the first one there come Sunday morning.

He paused, wondering what was next. Would he be around to go to church next week? Odd that he wasn't as worried as he thought he would be. It was as if this was where he needed to be so he could figure things out. Not with a friend or a colleague. Just here, right now next to one of his favorite people.

The screen door slammed, and he turned to see Fannie enter. Her face turned a pleasant color of pink.

"*Hallo*. Fancy seeing you here." His greeting seemed to fluster her even more, rare for her. "Have a seat." He gestured to the chair next to her *mammi*.

She kept her eye on him, as if he was a ghost. "What are you doing here?"

Frieda lifted her brows. "Well, I suppose that's one way to get a man's attention."

"I'm taking care of some things." He crossed one ankle over the opposite knee and straightened his pants leg cuff.

"Like what?"

Frieda shook her head. "You're as nosy as I am." She stood, and he noticed her limp. Her right leg seemed weaker since the last time he was there.

"I'll leave you two alone." She winked at Daniel and waddled to the kitchen.

"How long has that been going on?" He motioned to Frieda. "Her leg."

Fannie stared into the distance. "I guess I hadn't noticed."

"Or you didn't want to." It was obvious to him but then he was the doctor. "You should bring her in for an appointment."

"The doc is just fine with me." Frieda yelled from the kitchen.

"Well, now all the neighbors can hear that you need to go see Doc," Daniel called in to her.

Fannie leaned toward Daniel. "She says she's okay, but I don't think she's as comfortable as she claims to be."

"I can see that just by watching her stride. She should see an orthopedist. She's got too much going for her to let this get her down."

"She is still pretty active. Now I feel bad I didn't do something sooner." Fannie peeked in the kitchen and sighed.

"Don't be hard on yourself. When you live with someone every day, it's easy to miss things."

"Your *mamm* will be glad to see you." She gave him a small smile that lasted a little too long.

He cleared his throat. "I might be here a little longer than I'd expected."

"*Ach*, why's that?" Her head tilted to one side waiting for the answer he didn't want to give. "That's good, right?"

"No, it's not. You know how my hand shakes sometimes?" When he looked at her, he knew she understood but just didn't want to.

She sat up straight and furrowed her brow. "I don't understand."

"I won't be able to practice medicine because they consider me a liability." Hearing himself say those words out loud depressed him. It was really happening. He was about to lose his medical career. "All those years gone studying and working. Now, all for nothing."

"That's not true, Daniel. Look at Doc and what the community gives him for what he does for us. That can be you, Daniel. Your knowledge can't be wasted. You've done so much and worked so hard for that hospital. How can they do that to you?"

He leaned back, shaking his head at her naiveté. But hadn't he had the same thoughts just this morning?

She sensed that Daniel didn't want to talk about the hospital anymore. Then she remembered he was going to find out more about Lydia.

"Were you able to learn anything about Lydia—I mean, Misty—and the Troyers?"

"A bit." He repeated what Patience said about the Troyers being drug users and neglectful, but not actively abusive.

"I see." She folded her arms across her chest. "So they got tired of taking care of her and dropped her off in the community, knowing she'd be taken in by someone. So why did they come back for her?"

"Now." He made a placating motion with his hand. "We don't know that they dropped her off."

"They abandoned her." Fannie's voice was implacable. "So why do they want her back?"

Daniel shrugged. "Maybe they missed her."

Fannie rolled her eyes. "*Jah*. And I've missed picking up after you and cleaning your tools."

He grinned and teased her. "I thought you liked working with me."

She turned pink again and looked away. "Even if I do, we're talking about Lydia."

"Misty."

"Lydia." She spoke as if the matter was settled. And it seemed it was.

Chapter Thirty-Four

Fannie walked up the road to Daniel's *mamm's* house. A week had gone by since he'd visited her, and she could tell that Daniel had kept busy. The barn door hung straight again. The old tree was gone, and firewood was stacked on the porch, although with such warm days now, Margaret would be burning less.

Fannie was glad Daniel stayed with his *mamm*. He hadn't seen her since she'd returned from Ohio shortly after the storm. Fannie knew he was enjoying this time with his mother. But there was still mending to do, both within his family and around their family home.

They hadn't talked anymore about Lydia, but Fannie had caught glimpses of Daniel on his mobile phone, an intense expression on his face as he discussed something. She had a feeling it was about Lydia but couldn't say for sure. It eased her worry a bit knowing that even if Lydia's parents had abandoned her, Daniel wouldn't let her be forgotten.

He emerged from the barn and waved when he saw her.

"Your *mamm* must be glad you're here to help her with the farm." She smiled as he approached.

"She had a hard time leaving her family in Ohio and coming back here. This place doesn't give her peace. Too many bad memories, I think." He stared at the white house with black trim.

She followed his gaze. The gardens of flowers that used to be there were gone, another casualty of the storm.

"Our last meeting was good for my soul." He spoke more to himself than to her.

She followed him to the front porch. "I like this porch."

He shrugged. "*Mamm* likes to keep it decorated, though I never got why she bothers."

Fannie watched as Daniel used a hammer to nail down a few loose boards on the porch. Daniel seemed as comfortable with these tools as he was with his medical devices.

"Can I help you?" she asked.

He rocked back on his heels and pierced her with his brown eyes. "I'm not delivering babies or seeing patients. I'm swinging a hammer and painting."

"I can paint."

A smile tugged one side of his lips. "Okay, then. Get the paint and brushes from the barn."

They spent the next hour finishing up small tasks around the house and barn, and between the two of them they got twice as much done.

A buggy filled with children came down the pebbled lane. Margaret appeared on the porch to see who was arriving.

Fannie walked over to greet Elizabeth, Jake, and their

brood. "Looks like you have a full buggy this morning," she said. Not that any other day was different. Elizabeth didn't bother keeping track of all of them. She expected the elder children to do their parts in helping with the younger ones. Now, though, she looked on the verge of tears as she held a child in her lap.

"Fannie, we're in need of some help. Does Daniel have a minute?" Jake spoke before Elizabeth got a chance to open her mouth.

"What's the problem, Jake?" She watched their mass of children pile out of the buggy as she called for Daniel.

He came out of the barn and wiped off his hands with a towel. Daniel looked around at the brood of children who had suddenly inhabited his *mamm's* place.

"What seems to be the problem?" He studied each and every child but stopped when he saw the young boy sitting on his *mamm's* lap in the buggy.

"Looks like this one is in some pain." He bent down in front of the little guy and peered at him.

"Do you see anything?" Fannie was ready for whatever might come. Broken bones and fevers, cuts and hives, she'd helped him in stranger situations before. She moved to stand behind him, so she'd be nearby to help but not be in the way.

The young man opened his mouth wide as tears periodically ran down his cheeks.

"Can you get it out, Doctor?" Jake asked, though it sounded like more of a demand than a question. "Joseph's been moaning and crying about that fish bone in his throat since dinner last night."

"*Mamm*, run over to the community phone and call 911," Daniel said.

The boy's *daed* dropped his jaw and frowned. Margaret picked up her skirts and dashed away.

"Are you sure that's necessary, Daniel," the *daed* asked.

"Yes!" Daniel yelled and continued to give orders. "Fannie, I need some vinegar and an egg."

Fannie ran into the *haus* and looked through the cupboards until she found some vinegar and a basket of eggs. One of the boys followed her to carry the items. She handed him a teacup of water and the vinegar. "*Danke*." She nodded and they ran to Daniel.

Daniel pointed to the eldest boy. "Help me lift him up."

When they got the young man seated on the porch steps, Daniel stood in front of him. He poured some of the water onto the ground and added some vinegar to the cup. He stirred it with his finger then lifted it to the boy's lips. "Drink."

Joseph's eyes grew wide, but he swallowed obediently.

"I've got more vinegar if you need it." One of the girls offered and handed it to one of the bigger boys.

A small crowd had formed. Not just Joseph's family, but others from the community had gathered. Fannie didn't have time to puzzle out how everyone heard so quickly. Perhaps when Margaret called from the community phone, others overhead and came to offer help.

Joseph made a face as he downed the last of the vinegar water and handed the cup back to Daniel.

"Good," Daniel said to the patient. He cracked an egg into the now empty cup and handed it back to Joseph. "Now drink this in one gulp."

The patient shook his head. "Nuh uh."

"Is the bone still there?"

Joseph swallowed gingerly and his eyes filled with tears. He nodded.

"Then this has to go down or when the emergency medical vehicle arrives, they'll take you to the hospital and that means forceps down your throat."

Joseph sighed and straightened his shoulders, then reached for the teacup. His nose wrinkled, but he tipped the whole egg into his mouth. His cheeks bulged.

"Swallow." Daniel stood and folded his arms across his chest.

Joseph obeyed. He swallowed once. Then again. A smile spread across his face.

Fannie prayed for the best. "What happened?"

Daniel clapped his hands. "Good work every one. The vinegar softened the bone, and the egg unstuck it so he was able to swallow it."

The volunteer fire department came roaring down the road with lights whirling and turned down the lane.

Margaret trotted up and put an arm around Elizabeth's shoulders. She beamed and shook her head.

Jake walked over to Daniel and slapped him on the back. "I don't make much over fancy doctors, but you're an exception."

Joseph, then one of his brothers, then another, and then the interested onlookers all shook Daniel's hand or said a kind word. Joseph's father was last in line. "*Danke* again, Daniel. I didn't know you were such a good fisherman."

They chuckled and pumped hands. Then Elizabeth came and pinched Daniel's cheek. "*Danke*, Daniel, we're glad to have you here."

Daniel spoke to the fire crew who turned the truck around and retraced their way to the main road.

Fannie let out a breath. It was over and no one was seriously hurt. *Danke Gott* for small favors. She smiled. The most important thing of all was how the community all pulled together. Even with storm repairs still ongoing, people dropped what they were doing to offer help to a young man with a fish bone stuck in his throat. She watched people trickle back down the lane to their own homes and jobs.

When she turned around and saw Daniel, she realized how well he fit back in with his people, like he belonged. And somehow, he'd also found a place in her heart.

Chapter Thirty-Five

"Are you ready for the best mashed potatoes you've ever had?" Frieda turned from the stove with a steaming bowl in her hands.

Daniel grinned. The spread on the counter was almost full, with the last item still in the oven. This was to be a spring Thanksgiving. The *haus* was full of friends and neighbors celebrating and thanking God for surviving the storm and landslide.

After what they'd all been through and then him becoming a hero after helping Joseph with the fish bone fiasco, he found he couldn't say no to those who lived here. He'd been kept quite busy with rashes, colds, and ear infections. Another factor with running an Amish practice was not having to follow hospital procedures. He could use remedies that weren't as toxic as some pharmaceuticals and less abusive to the body. The vinegar and egg had been joined with other herbs in his arsenal of healing weapons. He'd found that he enjoyed using those remedies. He knew from here on out, whatever happened to his medical practice at the hospital, he would make a point to visit the community here more often.

Daniel noticed Fannie glancing at the door periodically. He knew she was hoping her *mamm* would show up, but she and Frieda were both stubborn. He felt he had no right to get involved, though a part of him longed to be able to step in and heal Fannie's hurts. He cleared his throat.

"Here you go, Daniel." Fannie set down a plate as she sat next to him.

They waited for the others to say grace before they started in on the delicious food. He couldn't remember the last time he'd had a homemade meal as good as this one.

"Ladies, to a wonderful meal with good company." He started to lift his glass but then thought better of it. He wasn't in the city or at a bar; he was amongst a group of people he respected, so he would be respectful toward them. "Thank you."

"Frieda," he whispered. "You are the best cook around." He winked, and she turned a nice color of pink.

"I heard that." Fannie set her fork down and lifted a brow.

She was just as good a cook as Frieda, but he liked to tease her. "You aren't so bad either." He grinned, and she ignored him. It was then he remembered how the Amish were about their recipes, and compliments were expected...along with a belch, although one wasn't required, at least not at his home when he was growing up.

"Take a joke. You know I've liked everything you've made." He nudged her with his arm. "Do we expect more deliveries any time soon?"

"Oh my, yes. I've been working day and night. It's as if babies are raining from heaven."

He smiled, glad he'd said the right thing. As he looked around at the neighbors, children, newborn babies, and parents, he realized how relaxed he was. There was no pager to answer or meetings to take up his day, and no working among so many who were just waiting for the weekend.

"You look content." He popped a piece of fried okra in his mouth as she ate a forkful of black-eyed peas.

"I do? I feel neutral, I guess. There are a lot of different thoughts floating around in my head that I don't know what to do with."

"Thoughts about what?" he asked.

"Thoughts about birthing babies, working at the bakery, saving money for a horse, and my *mamm* and *mammi*. Thoughts about Lydia and that her parents probably want her back for the money the state pays them for her food. Thoughts about the mudslide and the storm. Should I go on?"

He chuckled. "I forgot how many thoughts can fill a woman's brain. Emily used to tell me..." He trailed off. Fannie wouldn't want to hear what Emily said.

"*Jah*..."

He couldn't tell if Fannie's agreement was to his own inner thought about Emily or if she agreed that a woman's brain worked overtime.

As the meal came to an end, the women chatted and cleaned up the kitchen while the men talked out on the porch.

Fannie was working like a busy bee, as she called it. Daniel chuckled when her *mammi* actually made the sound like a bee, but it annoyed Fannie enough for her to go to another room until Frieda stopped.

Daniel started thinking about an Amish woman he wanted to check on after everyone left for the day. She was full term, and this pregnancy seemed different from her others, so he wanted to keep a close eye on her.

"Where are you going? Frieda's dinner didn't sit right with you?" Fannie leaned against the doorjamb. The color of the afternoon sun hit Fannie in just the right way. Layers of streaming light brought out her almond-shaped green eyes and the way one shoulder tilted ever so slightly.

"To check on a babe and its *mamm*. Care to go with me?"

He looked over at the kitchen to see if Fannie was done with one job and ready for another.

He caught her eye, and she smiled like a girl in a candy shop. She loved bringing life into the world. And so did he.

When they got to Naomi's home, she was more than thankful to have them there because her husband had not made it back yet from a trip to town for feed. He'd taken the other children so she could rest in peace.

Fannie placed her hands on her hips. "That husband of yours left you alone?"

"My neighbor was supposed to stop by, but I haven't heard from her. I sure am glad you're here."

Fannie fluffed some pillows around Naomi and had her lean against the headboard. "How does that feel? Comfortable?"

"*Nee*. I don't know, but whatever it is, it's uncomfortable."

"Where?"

"I feel like my stomach is too stretched, like a rubber band that's about to pop."

Daniel went through a number of questions, but none seemed to pinpoint the feeling she couldn't quite explain. He took out his stethoscope and listened intently but didn't hear anything out of order, except the one odd thing. "Mind if Fannie listens?"

The *mamm* nodded as Fannie rubbed her stomach and frowned. "She's tight as a drum."

He lifted a brow. "That's not unusual." Most women knew their bodies well enough to recognize abdominal tightness.

Fannie looked at her patient's belly again then reached for the stethoscope. She listened for a full minute until her eyes flew open, wide as saucers. "There are two!"

Daniel took the stethoscope and after he listened again, he nodded. "Two heartbeats, you're right. They're very close together. One is a quick echo of the other. Congratulations."

The mother-to-be held her large belly and looked dazed.

Fannie clapped her hands.

"That's wonderful news. You are blessed!"

The front door flew open, and Naomi's husband filled the opening. "I'm sorry! I got held up by a busload of tourists. I tried going through them, but they wouldn't stop with the pictures and the questions. I would have run them over if I didn't wait for them to finish."

"You're here in time, Mark," Fannie said. "And Naomi has some news for you."

A group of children threaded themselves through the doorway and surrounded their mother's bed.

Naomi's mouth curled into a smile. "It's twins."

The children burst into laughter and clapping.

Mark looked as if she'd told him she was having a hyena instead of a baby, but he gathered his composure quickly and rushed to Naomi's side. "Double the blessings!"

"*Jah*, and double the diapers." But Naomi seemed more at peace now that she knew what was going on and Mark was happy.

Chapter Thirty-Six

Spring was fading to summer. The tomato plants were setting green orbs. Young corn stalks poked their heads above ground. Daniel's leave was extended another two weeks while he underwent testing. Some of the more dire causes had been ruled out. Not Parkinson's. Not multiple sclerosis. Not a stroke. Not traumatic brain injury. He was less concerned about the shaking than he had been. In fact, he had been quite content in the community for the last several weeks, fixing up his childhood home and seeing the occasional patient.

He pulled weeds from the garden he'd planted. There were all kinds of ways to bring new life into the world, not just delivering babies. Planting seeds and reaping their bounty could be rewarding too.

A buggy came down the road. The parents of the twins he and Fannie had delivered not long ago, Naomi and Mark, pulled into the lane.

The family stepped out of the buggy and walked to the *haus* with their new babies.

Daniel's *mamm* emerged from the front door. "Well, good morning!" Margaret was beside herself to have little ones coming around. "And who are these lovely children?" She bent down to look at them and smiled when they got closer. "What darling children you have here."

"*Hallo*, Doc." The *daed* held out his hand and Daniel pumped it. "We wanted to stop by and give you some of our favorite meals."

One of their older daughters handed him a basket full of Amish-made goods. "I made the goodies in this basket. Hope you like them." Her blue eyes were solemn with the responsibility, but her smile was genuine.

"We also appreciated you delivering the babies, and we thought we'd name our little boy Daniel, if that's all right with you." Naomi glanced shyly at him from under her lashes. "*Jah*, Daniel and Ruth, after my *mammi*."

Margaret's face lit up as she clapped her hands together and smiled brightly. "That's *wunderbaar*!"

Daniel was surprised, but pleased as well. He'd been accepted by this family at least, even if not by the bishop.

Margaret continued to chat with the family, cooing at the babies and ruffling the hair of the older boys. She loved little ones, and Daniel knew she yearned for grandchildren close by. His siblings had all moved away, and she missed seeing the young ones. He knew she wanted Daniel to have a family of his own.

Mark came over and handed Daniel a wad of money. "I won't take no for an answer."

Daniel rubbed his chin and looked at him. "How about you give me the food, and you can keep that cash?"

Mark scratched his beard. "You sure?"

"I'm not a very good cook." Daniel couldn't have made a better deal; his stomach was starting to rumble.

A tap on his hand made Daniel turn his head. He looked down to see another of the family members. Large brown eyes met his gaze as the little girl looked up at him.

Daniel shook his head. "And you are?"

"Anna, and my *mamm* wants me to help with the babies." She swayed one way then the other with her hands behind her back without taking her eyes off him.

Daniel knew this was serious news, and he responded with the proper gravity. "Have you held them?"

"*Jah.*" She swished her blue dress around her legs and looked over at her *mamm*, who watched with a smile. "I know how to rub their backs until they burp."

A black and white blur in his peripheral vision drew Daniel's attention. He looked away to see a black and white dog running toward them. "Do you know this dog?" he asked.

"Him?" Mark pointed. "We're giving him to you if you'd like to have him. Fast runner, but the best thing about him is he's a good herder."

Daniel wasn't sure he wanted the dog but didn't want to be rude. That was until the dog stood, lurched, and chased after a rabbit with little effort.

"That's awful kind of you. I just might take him." Keeping the dog around might make him protective of the farm. Daniel was still unhappy about his *mamm* living at home alone, but she had been on her own for long enough to be accustomed to a solitary life, and she seemed to like where she was.

The family gathered in the buggy and rolled down the lane. He watched them go and didn't turn away until they dipped over the hill.

The kindness of the parents and pleasant attitude of the children brought back memories of the good times he'd had growing up.

"What are you thinking about, son?" *Mamm* came up behind him and mussed his hair like she had when he was a boy.

"Are you happy here, *Mamm*?" He looked over at her to see her eyes when she answered. To his surprise she was smiling.

"Actually, I am. Since your *daed* and I separated, I have had to put my trust in *Gott*. I always thought I trusted His will, but this tested my faith. He has taken care of me. I have all I need—friends, family, a *wunderbaar* community. And you coming around more often."

Daniel nodded. "I've been thinking about what you said, about how I need to forgive *daed*. I think you're right. I don't know if he'll ever charge, but I'm going to pray for him and leave everything that happened in God's hands."

His mother smiled. "I'm so glad to hear that, son."

She reached up and stroked his cheek. "I know you enjoy your work, but I hope you find someone who makes you happy. Like Fannie. You two seem to get along."

He held up a hand. "We're talking about you, not me." He should have thought quicker to avoid that one.

They stopped at her door and she kissed him on the cheek. "You deserve happiness. As much as I do. Maybe even more."

As he walked away, he thought about how this community was a good place to live. He liked it as a kid and always did when he came back for a visit. The air was clean, and the living was good. Delivering babies would be a change, if he left the hospital. He rubbed the hand that gave him nightmares and wondered where his place was, and if he could give up all he'd worked for.

Chapter Thirty-Seven

Fannie walked into the small clinic in time to hear Daniel say good-bye to a caller.

"My phone has been ringing off the wall." Daniel set the receiver down just as it jangled again. He scooped it back up. "Dr. Kauffman." He listened intently, scribbled a note, and hung up again.

"You've become a real dog lover." She nodded at the collie curled up next to Daniel's feet.

Daniel grinned at her and shrugged. "He's growing on me." He gave her an appraising glance. "He's not the only one I'm seeing differently these days."

She flushed and busied herself stocking his medical bag with supplies from the locked cabinet. Surely Daniel didn't mean that the way it sounded.

"Here are the visits for today." Daniel handed her a stack of papers with the names and addresses of the day's calls.

"Why so many?" She scanned them for hints of which supplies she needed to pack.

"We're in demand." He shrugged before turning away. "I'll get my jacket, and we'll head out."

She reached for the sterile gauze pads, added ace

bandages to the bag, then topical ointment. Amish weren't much for vaccines, but she knew Daniel often urged tetanus shots on patients with cuts from farm equipment. A few acquiesced. But not many. She reached for the serum and two syringes just as the phone rang again.

"Dr. Kauffman's office."

"Oh, Fannie, we need Doc here right away."

"Who is this?"

"Jake. I'm at the community phone. Elizabeth is at home. Joseph needs Doc again." Jake sounded more exasperated than worried.

She glanced at the already thick stack of calls and sighed. "What about Doc Rueben?"

"Who is it?" Daniel returned to the room, pulling his jacket over his shoulders.

She covered the mouthpiece. "Jake. He says Joseph needs you right away."

Daniel nodded. "I go when I'm called. I'm not sure if Doc is still making visits. Most of my calls are for situations more dire than what Doc likes to treat, anyway. Tell Jake we're on our way."

After delivering the message, she hung up. "Well, we better get moving then, or we'll be out until the sun goes down." She flipped the latch on the black bag.

Daniel whistled and the dog sat up. "In the truck, Captain."

The dog danced about under their feet until Daniel opened the clinic door. Captain then bounded to the truck and into the bed in a single leap.

Fannie laughed. "I see why you named him Captain. He's always ready."

"And he likes to be in charge." Daniel's low chuckle stirred something in Fannie's chest.

When they arrived at the farm, three dogs ran out to greet them. Captain gave a joyful bark and leaped from the truck and ran off with his friends.

Daniel and Fannie made their way to the front porch. A periodic cry and sniffle came closer as they knocked on the door.

"Doc, Fannie, come in, please. This way." Elizabeth held open the door.

As they walked in the kitchen, Fannie looked over to see something shiny and glinting on—or rather, in—a boy's nose. The closer she got, the more curious she was.

Daniel looked down, and Fannie followed his gaze. "Joseph has a fishing hook in his nose."

"Oh, my." Fannie saw that it had gone through one side and out the other. "Looks like you've been busy today." She smiled and squatted beside him. "How old are you?" He held up all ten fingers.

"We're going to help you feel better, *jah*?" She stood and looked at Daniel for direction and to tell him to hurry. This little one was going to really get upset in no time.

Fannie took Daniel's bag and pulled out the tools necessary for the extraction. Once the medicines and herbs were out and forceps lay ready, they began.

"Elizabeth, hold your boy for me." Daniel indicated the chair.

Elizabeth sat and gathered Joseph onto her lap. The front door slammed, and Jake appeared. "Glad to see you here."

Joseph whimpered and cried as they got him situated.

Fannie followed Daniel's directions as quickly as she could. She had seen fish hooks like this snag before. She wondered how Daniel would handle the situation.

He held out a hand. Fannie handed him the hydrogen peroxide and a square gauze pad. He daubed the moist pad, and the boy gasped as the peroxide bubbled and frothed on his nose.

"It's okay, *liebchen*." Elizabeth ran a hand along Joseph's arms to soothe him.

Fannie watched Daniel clip off the point of the hook.

"I'm going to pull the piece out. When I do, immediately put pressure on the wound to stop the bleeding." He looked up at Jake. "Has he had a tetanus shot?"

"*Nee*, we don't give shots, Doc. You know that."

"He'll need one, especially with all the rust on that old hook."

Jake considered then sighed. "I don't like it but if you think so..."

Fannie had seen similar fishing injuries, but none had been dealt with more quickly or as neatly as Daniel had just done.

Daniel nodded to his bag. "Fannie, will you grab that bag and find the medicine and a syringe?"

She opened the bag and pulled out the box that held the medication, but the box felt light. Too light. She rattled it, expecting—*nee*, praying—for one last vial in there to rattle around. Nothing.

"I don't see any that are for tetanus." She gave the bag to him, hoping he could find what she couldn't.

He grabbed it and rummaged through and then turned it upside down, pouring the contents of the bag all over the table. "This is time-sensitive. We need this shot done now."

"It's my fault." She blurted it out and froze when Daniel swung to her.

"What do you mean?"

"I was filling the bag when Jake called and interrupted me. I forgot to add the tetanus serum."

His face filled with dismay and something else she couldn't identify. Disappointment? In her. "What can I do?" Her voice quivered a bit, and she cleared her throat.

His lips tightened, and he gazed around the room. Joseph still sniffling. Elizabeth with her forehead creased with worry. Jake with his arms folded across his chest. "They'll have to ride with us back to the clinic."

Jake opened his mouth, but Daniel held up a hand. "I know most Amish don't want to use medical science, but in this case it can turn into a life-or-death situation. I'm sorry I don't have the tetanus shot with me. That's never happened before, and believe me when I say I'll make sure it doesn't happen again."

Fannie kept her eyes from his face, afraid of the censure she'd see there.

Jake frowned with frustration. "I don't know that I want this done to my son. It's *Gott's* will if Joseph gets the illness or not."

Daniel threw his hands up and paced in a tight circle. "How can I make you understand?"

Fannie interrupted and spoke directly to Jake. "That's up to you, but for your son's sake I wish you'd take Doc's advice. He's already helped Joseph once. He wouldn't recommend it if it wasn't necessary. Perhaps it is *Gott*'s will that Joseph have the shot and avoid the illness. He is prone to accidents. This would help keep him safe in the future, especially if Dr. Kauffman wasn't nearby."

The *daed* grunted and looked over at his wife. She nodded and he shrugged. "*Aye*, then."

Fannie let out a breath and smiled at Daniel.

He smiled back.

They bundled everyone into the back of the truck. Joseph sat in the front between Fannie and Daniel.

"I'm so sorry, Daniel," she murmured.

He reached across Joseph and gave her hand a squeeze. "It will be fine. The extra half-hour is nothing. He'd probably wait that long for the shot in the emergency room. I over-reacted."

"It won't happen again." She spoke softly, unable to look at him.

"I know." He gave her hand another squeeze and then let go. "I know it won't."

Once at the office Daniel gave Joseph the shot. He only whimpered.

"Here." Daniel pulled a bill from his wallet and handed it to the young boy. "Go over to the general store. You all deserve a treat."

Joseph rushed out, waving the bill. Fannie laughed as his siblings called to him to slow down as they hurried after him. Jake and Elizabeth followed at a slower pace after thanking Daniel again. They declined his offer to drive them back to the farm, saying they wanted to walk and enjoy the spring day.

Fannie had to admit it was a lovely day. She'd been so wrapped up in the calls they had to make that she hadn't even noticed the sunlight falling through the clouds to the green earth.

Daniel locked the clinic door behind the family and turned to Fannie. "We best get back to work or—" His phone rang, interrupting him. He glanced at the little screen then his forehead creased. "Hello? Patience?" He looked at Fannie for a brief instant then turned away. He listened for a long minute, then thanked his caller and disconnected.

"Is everything all right?" Fannie asked. She'd never seen Daniel so intense in a conversation with so few words.

His lips thinned as he nodded. "I think so."

Fannie crinkled her brow. "What's going on?"

"Remember Patience, the woman who was helping me find out about Misty's parents? She talked to them about why they abandoned her, though they keep insisting she ran off in the storm."

"And?" Against her better judgment Fannie found herself hungry for details about the little girl.

"The Troyers paid Patience a visit today. She called Mrs. Wurtemberg and then me."

Something flickered in Fannie's chest. If she didn't know better, she'd think it was hope.

"The Troyers have decided they can't take care of Misty and live the way they want to. They decided to give her up for adoption."

Disbelief collided with joy, and Fannie fought to keep a calm expression. "What does that mean?"

"It means she's coming back to the Lapps'!" He picked Fannie up and swung her in a circle. "It means we'll get to see her again. It means she won't be living in a dingy house with drug users and other people who might hurt her or victimize her. It means she'll be safe."

Fannie allowed herself to sink into Daniel's arms, to enjoy the sensation of feeling cared for and secure in someone's embrace. This must be what Lydia felt when Daniel found her that first day.

Fannie burst into tears.

Daniel set her down. "What's wrong? This is good news."

Fannie nodded. "*Jah*, I know it is." She sniffled. "That's why I'm crying; I'm so happy for Lydia."

"Misty." He said it with the half-grin she used to find so irritating.

"Lydia."

His face fell for a brief moment. "I guess it will be up to the child herself and the Lapps what name she goes by."

Fannie had no reply for that. Of course, neither she nor Daniel had a say in anything pertaining to Lydia. They weren't part of Lydia's family. Not part of any family really. Both of them were from fractured families. His parents had separated, and her *mamm* and *mammi* couldn't live in the same house.

Of course, she and Daniel had no understanding, so the thought of being a family was silly at best and downright ridiculous at worst. So she let Daniel have the last word and turned away from him so he wouldn't see her tears of happiness turn to tears of sorrow.

Chapter Thirty-Eight

"The chief of staff is waiting for you in his office."

Daniel turned around to see who was behind him. "Cindy."

She grinned in a way he couldn't decipher. Her forced smile put Daniel on guard.

She put one hand on her hip and gave him a cool smile. "How are you, Daniel?"

He ran a hand through his hair and spoke warily. "Fine. I think I'm fine."

He felt awkward, like he owed her something, even though their relationship ended before it started. He was sorry if he'd hurt her and waited for the tongue lashing that he probably deserved, wanting to get it over with.

She waved a hand with a shiny diamond on her ring finger. "No worries, I'm in good hands."

He smiled with surprise and a little relief. "Congratulations, who's the lucky guy?"

"Greg, in accounting. It happened so fast, but we both just knew."

"I wish you the best."

She nodded. "Yeah, you too."

With that he walked away to face what he'd been avoiding for far too long. He took in a breath and walked in the secretary's office.

"Hey Kate, is Dr. Ambrose in?"

She stopped typing and gave him a smile.

"Daniel, good to see you. I hear you've been doctoring the Amish instead of us these days."

"As it turns out, yeah, it's been busy. And you?"

She waved a hand. "Same old. You know, I have an aunt who lives in that group, Mary Stoltzfus."

He'd treated Mrs. Stoltzfus for an infected corn on her foot just the other day, but he couldn't tell Kate that. Patient privacy rules were ingrained in him. He settled for something vague. "She's a nice lady."

"Well, I'll be sure and tell her you said so."

He nodded as she opened the door for him, and he took a deep breath. He rubbed his shaky hand, prayed for wisdom, and walked through the door to decide his future.

Thirty minutes later Daniel walked out of the hospital and inhaled the fresh air. The aromas of the hospital, so much a part of his life for the last ten years, wafted away like fog over the pond. This was the last time he'd be here as a doctor, at least in this hospital.

He was almost to the car when he decided to turn around and make one more visit. He hadn't talked to Jack since he'd been away in the community. He owed him as least a decent good-bye, even though the phone lines and roads ran both ways. Jack hadn't made any effort either.

Daniel peeked in Jack's door to see him talking on the phone. When Daniel walked in and sat in the chair across from his desk, Jack turned around and did a double take. "I'll call you back," he said into the phone and hung up.

"Surprised to see me?" Daniel asked.

"As a matter of fact, I am. I thought you were done with this place."

"I'm settling things up."

Jack leaned back in his chair and gave him an appraising look. "I figured you'd be here as long as me. I thought we'd leave together, start our own practice."

"I thought so too at one time," Daniel admitted. "This hasn't ended the way I expected. It wasn't my choice. At least I'll still be working, just not here."

"And where will you be?" Jack tapped his pencil on his desk, obviously interested.

"With the community."

Jack grinned. "I'd heard rumors. Well, best of luck to you." A light lit on his phone. "Duty calls." He stood, and Daniel did the same.

"Good to see you." He reached out his hand, and Jack reciprocated.

"Thanks for stopping by."

Daniel nodded and turned to leave. And when he looked back through the window in the door, Jack was watching him go. Daniel felt lighter, not doubting for a minute that this was what he needed to do. He often wondered if working in the hospital was truly fulfilling the purpose God had for him, the purpose that made him leave the community to pursue more education. Now God was redeeming everything he thought he'd lost.

The choices he'd made were bringing him back to more than he thought possible. Home was where God wanted him, with the people he'd grown up with—and, he hoped, the woman he loved.

Chapter Thirty-Nine

Fannie went out to the well to bring more water to Frieda. She was making *schnitzel* for the Lapps, who were going to Social Services to make some decisions that would lead to Lydia officially becoming part of their family.

Fannie tried to be happy that Lydia would have a real home. But her heart ached at the same time.

Fannie brought the bucket into the kitchen just as a knock sounded at the front door. "*Mammi*, get the water, I'll get the door."

When she reached for the door handle, it opened, and her *Mamm* stood there.

Fannie's mouth dropped, and she moved forward to give her *Mamm* a hug. "I didn't know if you'd come when I didn't hear from you. Come in."

Frieda came in and stopped short. "Well, I'll be, look what the buggy drug in."

Fannie held her breath, unsure how they would respond to each other. The clock ticked and neither spoke; they just looked at each other.

"Well, are you coming in or not?" Frieda put a hand on her hip and waited.

"Due to the letter you sent, I accept your offer to come back and visit." Verna pulled out a bottle of ginger root. "Homemade from my garden."

Frieda didn't have the touch for gardening, and *Mamm* didn't do that well making *schnitzel*, so they were a perfect match. They just didn't know it sometimes.

"I'm headed to the kitchen right behind you." Fannie couldn't help but join in. She always learned a thing or two from them.

The sound of Daniel's car surprised her, as she didn't think he'd come this early. She walked out of the *haus* and approached him in the car.

"I'm surprised to see you." When she got a good look at him she noticed his strong chin pushed out, a sign he was worried or upset. "Bad day?" She hoped it wasn't, not with the reunion the ladies just had.

"I'm not sure, but no, I think it was a good day."

"What do you mean?"

"I'm unemployed." He looked straight out through the car window, and she couldn't read his mood.

"I'm sorry, Daniel." She reached in the window and put a hand on his arm. She had mixed feelings. He'd lost his income, and she hoped he might work here. Even more, she hoped he would stay here. With her. The thought slammed her in the chest. She loved Daniel. But he had medical school loans to pay still. There was no way he could stay here with her. She shamed herself for the selfish thought and focused on Daniel. "What happened?"

He rubbed his arm, then looked at her. "I have a thyroid condition. That's why my hand trembles. It's not common in men, which is why it took so long to figure out what was wrong. But it's treatable with medications."

"But that's *wunderbaar*!" she exclaimed. "You can still practice medicine then?"

He nodded. "It's all in the open now. I have nothing to hide. That much is good. No more wondering when the tremor will start up. The ironic thing about it is, the chief of staff said he'd work with me if I chose to stay."

"But you said you were unemployed." Confusion clouded her mind. "I don't understand. That's good news." For one brief second she hoped he hadn't said yes, then stopped her thoughts. "But you didn't agree to come back?"

He climbed out of the car, looked long and hard into her eyes, and then took her hand. "I declined his offer."

She forced her breathing to slow down. "I'm so selfish. I was hoping that you wouldn't go back."

"We're in agreement then." He squeezed her hand. "So I just have to set up a practice, after I talk to Doc Rueben. And the bishop. He said he'd never let me back."

She wondered why he thought it was such an issue. "Well, that was before you were a doctor and before Doc Rueben wanted to slow down. You don't have to worry about folks accepting you, not with half a dozen Amish women on your side."

He grinned.

"Folks are getting a little uneasy about Doc. You know it's time he quit seeing patients and spent more time with his wife and grandchildren."

Daniel looked over at her. "Are you telling me to take care of Doc so I can be the doctor?"

She shrugged. "Well, *jah*, maybe you could work together for a time."

"I was thinking of opening a birthing center." He kept his eyes forward, which gave her time to soak that in. "To start with. Then slowly see other patients too, if Doc and the bishop both agree."

He drew a deep breath and gazed into her face. His brown eyes brimmed with emotion, and her heart quickened. "Even more important, I'd like to work with you, delivering babies just like we've done since I came back. In fact, I'd like to do a lot more than work together."

He put his hands on her cheeks and ran a thumb along each cheekbone. "It took us a long time to get here, but now that we are, would you like to be married to an Amish doctor?"

A swell of emotions made her heart race, but she managed to nod. "*Jah*, I think I would like that."

His kiss was firm, yet gentle and tender. He kissed her with authority, and she pulled away breathless.

"Oh, Daniel."

His brown eyes brimmed with love. "I also want us to talk to Mrs. Wurtemberg about becoming Lydia's foster parents."

Her own eyes filled with tears, and she swallowed hard.

"Would that be okay with you, if we became an instant family?"

She nodded, and he kissed her again.

"I love you, Fannie. Are you sure you can put up with me and my tremor and a child and a medical practice? It's a lot of change at once."

She pushed him back an inch or two so she could look into his eyes, determined to have the last word this time. "It's all I ever wished for."

Excerpt From

Annie's Truth

Prologue

THE BRIGHT MOON illuminated the velvet sky. Shafts of corn swayed in the soft, warm breeze as if alive, dancing a waltz in the huge ten-acre field. The cries from a pack of coyotes erupted through the nearby hills surrounding the Shenandoah Valley.

Amos Beiler made his way through the rows of ripe corn as the pups howled an off-kilter tune along with the group. Amos followed a different cry—that of a human babe, the sobs weak and intermittent, nearly drowned out by the louder yelp of the coyotes.

He used his shotgun to slash his way through the six-foot stalks in a maze of never-ending rows until a small whimper close by made him stop. He turned to his right and looked down a stretch of dirt that led to his farmhouse a good mile away. He'd come to protect his livestock from the coyotes, but finding their prey was his new goal.

Another sputter from the next line over caught his attention. He moved quickly, not wanting to lose sight of the area where the sound came from. Cornstalks shadowed the dirt path that led him closer to the child. Now in bouts of darkness, he listened with an attentive ear to any tiny sound. A frog croaked. The wind rustled through the corn leaves. Another curt howl sounded. All made him pause, listen, and discern.

Another wail from the babe made him step quickly, running through the dark aisle of soil. Finally he caught a glimpse of movement; something white flashed from the ground. As he neared, he saw a colorless blanket. He unwrapped it to find a newborn inside. As he lifted the small bundle to his chest, a sense of urgency stirred up in him. The need for protection set him into action.

The coyotes' song ended. They were on the hunt now, looking for the prize he'd found. They were downwind of him, sure to have his scent and that of the child.

Carrying the gun with one hand and the babe close to his shoulder, he cradled its head in his palm and hurried toward the house. He looked behind him only once and saw motion out of the corner of his eye. The wind played tricks on him that he dared not allow to fool him. The faster he walked, the farther away the house seemed.

When Amos finally reached a window on the side of the house, he lifted the gun and banged one time, hard. He dropped to his knee and scanned the field. One, two, four pairs of yellow eyes fell upon him. He set the crying babe on the ground behind him. Then he steadied his gun.

Chapter One

THE DINNER BELL rang just as one of the milk cows slapped Annie's *kapp* with its tail. Now she was late for the evening meal. She pulled the black *kapp* off her head. When Maggie swatted Annie, the pins were knocked loose. She wiped off the dirt and cow manure then hastily twisted up her hair into a bun and pulled the *kapp* over her mess of hair.

"Need some help?" John Yoder's dark eyes smiled at her.

She jumped at the sight of him looking down at her with a grin. "*Nee*, I can finish up."

Her *mamm* would scold her for her tardiness and her unruly hair, so she quickly grabbed two containers of milk, clutching them to her chest. When she turned around, John was removing the cups from the Guernsey's udders.

"*Danke*. The boys must have missed a couple." The cover of one of the containers lifted, causing milk to spill out onto her black dress. Annie wiped her hand on her white apron. Frustration bubbled up and burst out in an irritated groan.

"Now what?" John opened the barn door and shut it behind them.

Annie pointed to the milk stain and slowed her walk so he could catch up. Her *mamm* wouldn't be as upset with her if she saw Annie with John.

"I spilled on myself, my hair's a mess, and I'm late." She juggled the containers to keep them in place as she walked.

John's smile never left, just tipped to the side while she listed her worries. "You're never late."

"You will be too if you keep talking to me." The milk sloshed around in the containers as she adjusted them again. "Taking the long way home?"

"*Jah*, thought I'd come by to say *hallo*." He took one from her then reached for the other.

She turned slightly so he couldn't reach the second bottle. "I've got this one."

"Suit yourself." He shrugged as his grin widened.

They walked together toward their houses, which were down the path from one another, divided by a dozen trees. John was three the day Annie was born and had been a part of her life more than her own brothers were at times. His brown hair brushed his collar as he walked with her, holding back to keep in step with Annie.

"Aren't you late to help with cooking?" He nodded toward her white clapboard house. A birdfeeder was hung at the far end of the porch, which had a peaked black roof, and daisies filled her *mamm*'s flower garden in front of the house. *Mamm* created a colorful greeting of flora for every season.

She shook her head. "*Nee*, Eli's helping the Lapps, so I'm helping the boys with milking. What were you doing, cutting tobacco?"

He nodded. "Nice day for it too. The sun was bright, but there was a breeze that kept us cool." He lifted his strong, handsome face toward the sunshine and took in a deep breath.

He was just trying to irritate her, so she ignored his jab. John knew she preferred being outdoors and that she would trade places with him in an instant. When the time was right she would help with the tobacco harvesting and, along with many others, would then prepare the meal after the task was done.

"It looked warm outside to me." She took the milk from him and kept walking. The last of the warm summer days were coming to an end, and soon it would be time for fall harvesting.

They reached the trail that led to John's home on the far side of a stand of tall oak trees. "Not as hot as in the kitchen." He snapped his suspenders and turned onto the trail leading away from her.

"John Yoder..." was all she could say this close to her *daed*'s ears. She watched him continue on down the roughed-out dirt lane thinking of what she would have said if she could. Her gaze took in the many acres of barley, corn, and oat crops and then moved to the Virginia mountainside beyond, where the promise of fall peeked out between the sea of green.

Annie walked up the wooden stairs and into the kitchen. The room was simple and white, uncluttered. A long table and chairs took over the middle of the large room, and rag rugs of blue and emerald added color and softness. For a unique moment it was silent.

"Annie?" Her *mamm*'s voice made her worry again about being late, with a soiled dress and unkempt hair.

Her tall, slender *mamm* stopped picking up the biscuits from a baking pan and placed both hands on the counter. She let out a breath when Annie came into the kitchen.

"*Ach*, good, you brought the milk." *Mamm*'s tired gaze fell on Annie.

"I was talking with John." She opened the cooler door and placed the milk on the shelf.

Her *mamm*'s smile told Annie she wasn't late after all, so she continued. "He said it was a good day for baling."

Hanna and her brother strolled in, and he grabbed a biscuit, creating a distraction that allowed Annie time to twist her hair up and curl it into a tight bun. A tap from their *mamm*'s hand made her son drop the biscuit back into the basket with the rest.

"I'm so hungry." Thomas's dark freckles on his pudgy face contrasted to his light hair and skin, so unlike Annie's olive-colored complexion, which was more like their *daed*'s.

She tousled his hair. "You are always the first one to dinner and the last one to leave."

"I'm a growing child. Right, *Mamm*?" Thomas took the basket of biscuits to the table and set them next to his plate.

"That you are. Now go sit down and wait for the others." *Mamm* placed a handful of biscuits in the breadbox and brushed her hands off on her white apron.

While they waited for the others to wash up, she addressed Annie. "John walked you out this morning and walked you home?"

"Like he has most every day of my life." Annie's voice almost reached the edge into sarcasm, but she smiled to make light of it. Didn't her *mamm* know that her obvious nudging turned Annie away from John, not toward him?

Hanna had been quiet, listening, and walked over to Annie. "Should we ask *Mamm* if we can look in our chests in the attic?"

Annie peered over Hanna's shoulder at *Mamm*. "*Jah*, but let's wait until after supper."

Her *mamm*'s brow lifted just as the buzz of her family coming into the room sidetracked her attention from Annie and Hanna. The younger ones were restless with hunger, and the older siblings talked amongst themselves. Frieda, Hanna, Augustus, Eli, Thomas, and Samuel all sat in the same chairs they were always in, and Annie took her assigned seat with the rest.

Her *daed* sat at the head of the table and waited with watchful eyes until everyone was quiet. When Amos folded his hands, all followed suit, and they all said silent grace.

Geef ons heden ons dagelijks brood. Give us this day our daily bread. Amen. Annie thought the words then kept her eyes closed until she heard movement from the others.

Amos passed the food to his right until it made a full circle back to him.

"We've almost finished with the Lapps's tobacco field," Annie's oldest brother, Eli, informed Amos. He and Hanna had *Mamm*'s silky blond hair and blue eyes, but Hanna didn't have her disposition.

Amos nodded and lifted a bite of chicken to his mouth.

Eli leaned toward Amos. "I can then tend to our barley day after tomorrow."

Amos spoke without looking at his son. "You will work the Lapps's land until they say you are finished. Not before."

The gleam in Eli's dark eyes faded as he took up his fork. "*Jah*, *Daed*."

Mamm spoke then. "It's an honor you are able to help

them while their *daed* recovers." She shifted her attention to her husband. "Have you heard how Ephraim is healing?"

Amos continued to eat as he spoke to her *mamm*. "His back is mending. It's his worrisome wife that keeps him laid up."

"*Ach*, I'd probably do the same if it were you." *Mamm* waited a moment until *Daed*'s mouth lifted into a half smile.

He gave the table a smack to stop Frieda from tempting Thomas with another biscuit. "The boy can help himself without your teasing him."

She set their hands in her lap. "*Jah*, *Daed*."

He nodded for them to eat again. Conversation was uncommon during meals, so Annie let her mind wander. Harvest season was approaching, and the excitement of upcoming weddings was on everyone's mind. Although the courtship was to be kept quiet, most knew which couples would most likely be married in the coming months.

Annie's mind went to John, the one she knew her parents, as well as his, would expect her to be with. Although she had feelings for him, she wished her spouse would not be chosen for her. It had changed her relationship with him just knowing what their expectations were. He had been her best friend, but she now kept him at bay, hoping for more time before the pressure became too great and they were forced to marry.

She put the palm of her hand to her forehead, resting there with thoughts of who else she could possibly be with from their community. Names went through her mind, but not one appealed to her in the same way John did.

Hanna nudged Annie as everyone began to clear the

table. Annie's mind rushed back to the present. She knew why Hanna wanted her attention. She was thinking about the upcoming nuptials too. Their wedding chests gave them promise for their own special day.

"Let's ask *Mamm*." Hanna's eyes shone with excitement. Annie felt a lift in her spirits at the thought of having the privilege to rummage through their special treasures. She looked at her *mamm* laughing at her brother's story of his britches getting caught on the Lapps's fence. Her smile faded when he showed her the hole the wire made, which she would be mending that evening.

"You ask her," Annie urged.

Hanna was the closest to Annie's age and her confidante, as she was Hanna's. "After dinner." Hanna got up from her chair to help.

Frieda started the hand pump as the others gathered the dishes and put away the extra food. Once the dishes were cleaned and dried, Hanna and Annie went to their *mamm*, who stacked plates in the cupboard as the girls walked over to her.

"What do you want to ask me?" *Mamm* continued with the dishes until the last plate was put away.

Hanna and Annie looked at one another. Annie furrowed her brows to make Hanna talk.

"We'd like to see our hope chests."

"It's a long while from any weddings being published." *Mamm* placed a hand on the counter and studied them. "Okay, then. But after your lessons are done."

Hanna grabbed Annie's hand, and they walked quickly from the kitchen. "*Jah*, *Mamm*," they said in unison. Annie hadn't looked through her chest since she'd given up the doll her *mamm* had made for her. Since it was her first, Annie had chosen to store it after receiving another from her aunt.

Hanna urged Annie to stop doing homework after she completed hers, but Annie wouldn't go until she'd finished her story. Finally the girls ran up the wooden stairs to the attic. Hanna grabbed the metal doorknob and pushed on the door to open it. The door creaked in the darkness, and Annie held the kerosene lamp up to examine the room before entering. It looked exactly the same as the last time she'd been there.

A chest of drawers held baby clothes, and beside it stood a cabinet full of documents and paperwork *Daed* kept but never seemed to use. Special dresses and a bonnet hung on the far side of the room alongside a box of old toys her *daed* and Eli had made.

The girls spotted the chests lined up next to one another, where they would remain until their owners were married. Amos had made each of his girls one in which to keep their sentimental belongings. One day, when they had their own homes, they would have a memory of their *daed* and the things they held dear during their childhood.

Annie ran to the last one. Amos had lined them up according to age, so Hanna's was right next to Annie's. "You first," Annie told Hanna.

"*Nee*, you." Hanna moved closer to Annie and watched her lift the heavy wooden lid. "I can't wait." Hanna went to her chest and opened it as well. "*Ach*, I'd forgotten." Hanna reached for the doll *Mamm* had made for her.

Annie grabbed hers, and they examined them together, just alike and equally worn. "I loved this doll! I had forgotten how much I played with it when I was a child."

The black bonnet was torn around the back, and the hay stuffing peeked out the back of the doll's dress.

"Mine is tattered as well. I'm glad we put them away when we did, or there would be nothing left of them." Hanna glanced at Annie's doll.

Annie placed the doll in her lap and pulled out her wedding quilt, the one of many colors. Hanna's was a box design, and Annie's was circles within circles, resembling the circle of life. She ran her hand across the beautifully stitched material and admired her *mamm*'s handiwork. When she looked up, Hanna was doing the same.

Their eyes met. "Hold yours up so I can see." Hanna's voice was soft and breathy. "It's beautiful, Annie. You're lucky to be closer to marrying than me."

Annie tilted her head and turned the quilt to face her. "I don't feel ready."

Hanna's brows drew together in question. "Why? You've always known you'll be with John. And he is a handsome one." She grinned. "I'll take him off your hands."

Annie tried to force a smile. "Why has everyone chosen my spouse for me?"

Hanna put her quilt back into the chest. "Don't let your mind wander. Just be happy with the way things are."

Annie fell silent, in thought. "Questioning is how we find the truth."

"The truth has already been found." Hanna reached for her family Bible as she spoke.

Annie nodded, humbled, and looked for her special Bible. She moved a carved toy Eli had made for her and a book her *mamm* had given to her. Finally, at the very bottom, she found a Bible the minister gave her. As she opened it up, she skimmed through the flimsy pages. She went to the very front of the book and smiled when she saw how she had written her name as a young girl. The letters were varied sizes and uneven.

Her *mamm*'s and *daed*'s names were both written under hers, their dates of birth, and a list of her brothers and sisters under that. Births and other dates of additional relatives proceeded on to the next page, including the dates of their marriages. Annie flipped back to the first page and noticed the day of her birth was missing. Only the year was written; the day did not precede it, only the month.

"Hanna, come look." Annie handed her the Bible and searched her sister's face for some sign that she knew the reason for the omission. Annie thought back to the days her family recognized her birthday—one in particular.

Birthdays were often celebrated after church service on Sundays when everyone was already together and they wouldn't take time away from daily chores during the week. This being tradition, Annie didn't think much of the exact date of her birth. Thoughts of self were discouraged. Everyone was treated equally so as to prevent pride.

On Annie's thirteenth birthday she had been surprised by her family and friends with a party. A cake with thirteen candles was brought out, and gifts were given. Her brother had made her a handmade wooden box, and her sister, a picture of flowers. Other useful gifts such as nonperishable food and fancy soaps made by her aunt in the shape of animals piled up on the picnic table next to a half-eaten cake.

The best gift was from John. He had taken an orange crate and decorated it with his wood-burning tools. It was filled with small, flat wooden figures of every significant person in her life. The time and care he had put into the gift had touched Annie. She treated the present with such care she had thought it wise to store it in her hope chest. Now Annie wished she had enjoyed the box more.

She searched for it now and found the pieces scattered throughout the bottom of the chest. She picked up the wooden figures one by one, examined them, and put them in the box. Although they all looked alike, as no graven images were permitted, she used her imagination to pick out each person. Frieda, Hanna, Augustus, Eli, Thomas, and Samuel were all accounted for, then *Mamm* and her *daed*, her *mammi* and *dawdi*—grandparents—then John and her. All of the boy figures looked the same as well except for their height, facial hair, and a hat her *dawdi* always wore.

She'd envision John's figure to be the exception. He had a thick head of black hair and always wore it a bit longer than he should. He could always get away with such things due to his charismatic personality. That was something not encouraged, so not often seen in their community.

Annie ran a finger along the small wooden likeness of John and wondered if she shouldn't dismiss him so readily. As a friend she adored him, but the thought of marrying him annoyed her. But did that feeling come because of him, or was it her?

Hanna's sigh brought Annie back to the moment. Hanna looked from her Bible to Annie's. "That's odd, isn't it?"

Annie turned a crisp page and stared at the words again. "I wonder if *Mamm* simply didn't remember to fill in the day."

Hanna frowned. "It's not like *Mamm* to forget to do anything like this."

Annie didn't want to believe that *Mamm* forgot, and Hanna was right in that their *mamm* never left anything undone, especially when it came to her children. "I'm sure there's a reason."

"The only thing left to do is ask." Hanna closed the Bible and handed it to Annie.

Annie took the black book, its pages edged with light gold.

"Don't you want to?" Hanna grasped her hands together and set them on her knees.

"*Jah*, I do." Annie stroked the top of the golden pages with her finger. "And then I don't."

Hanna grunted. "Well, that's silly."

Annie stopped and took the Bible in both hands. "But I have a strange feeling." Annie squeezed the Good Book. "Maybe it's better if I don't know."

Glossary

ach—oh
aye—yes
daed—father
danke—thank you
dawdi—grandfather
Englischer—non-Amish person
Gott—God
gut—good
hallo—hello
haus—house
jah—yes
kapp—hat
liebchen—a term of endearment
mamm—mother
mammi—grandmother
Meidung—shunning
nee—no
Ordnung—a set of rules
wille—will
wunderbaar—wonderful
ye—you